Arkady dashed up the escalator in time to see Philippa disappear through the door to the parking decks. She was moving fast, like someone in a nightmare.

He followed her to the entrance to the parking deck where he saw her look about quickly, then climb into the seat of a hovercraft. Within seconds, the craft rose on its pressor beam. Arkady set off after her, but before he'd covered half the lot, Philippa had deftly turned about and raced down the ramp. He slowed to a stop. Looking down at the name on the parking space, he saw *Yamoto*.

Raising his eyes, he scanned the main road and caught the gleam of sunlight on the vehicle's bubble as it sped away. Arkady stood silently, trying to comprehend the fact that Philippa Bidding—cool, collected, and one of Alphorion's elite—had just stolen the Yamoto family's hovercraft.

Other books in the **PLANET BUILDERS** series:

#1 Mountain of Stolen Dreams
#2 Night of Ghosts and Lightning

PLANET BUILDERS

REBEL FROM ALPHORION

Robyn Tallis

IVY BOOKS • NEW YORK

With thanks to Bruce Coville, Debra Doyle,
Jim Macdonald, and Sherwood Smith—
who built the planet.

To Peter and Mary Liera
Thanks for your patience!

Ivy Books
Published by Ballantine Books

Produced by Butterfield Press, Inc.
133 Fifth Avenue
New York, New York 10003

Library of Congress Catalog Card Number: 88-91243

ISBN: 8041-0205-8

Manufactured in the United States

First Edition: February 1989

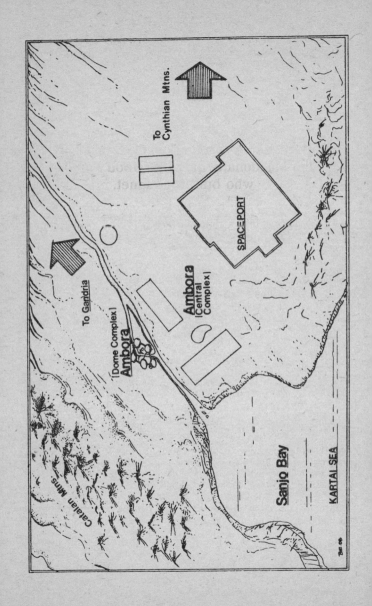

ONE

DID YOU SEE THAT?

Sixteen-year-old Will Mornette cranked his hover-scooter into high and sped down the road after his friends. Zach Yamoto was driving the other craft; all that was visible of him was his shoulder-length brown hair. Seated behind Zach was tall, black-haired Sean Matthews—unofficial leader of the third cohort students at Bradbury School, and organizer of this secret expedition.

Zach veered around a corner at top speed. Following more slowly, Will leaned into the wind cautiously. His heart was pounding. Too many strange distractions at too high a speed for a guy raised on a low-gravity dome world: wind in the face, open sky, and worst of all, this heavy gravity. At .98 of Earth Standard, most of the colonists on this newly settled planet called Gauguin found the gravity comfortable. It was six times what Will was used to, and every move he made threatened his

1

balance. And it didn't help, Will thought grimly, that he was also taller than anyone else—two meters, and still growing.

Zach skirted another tight corner and whizzed up the road. Will's hands gripped the steering bars, his stomach clenched as he followed.

Early-morning light from Gaugin's fierce blue sun flashed at him between the branches of a huge vellkul tree, then the light was behind him, hot on his shoulder blades, as he reached the crossroads.

At least now there's not much danger of meeting other traffic, Will thought. Then he frowned at the road blurring past. *Though if Sean's right, and we're seen by whoever made that camp, the danger won't be just my crashing from bad driving.*

Ahead, Sean suddenly stuck his hand out. Zach slowed his scooter. Will carefully cut speed, guiding his craft next to Zach's. Sean didn't wait for the hovercraft's pressor beam to dissipate; he jumped off the back of Zach's scooter and moved around to the front of the two vehicles, his green eyes narrowed as he studied his friends' faces.

"I was just thinking," Sean said wryly, "that this was too easy."

Puzzled, Will said, "I told you when you called— I've got early shift free today. School at midshift and drudge late shift." *Drudge* was the first term Will had learned on coming to Gauguin: It stood for the voluntary community service that all colonists fifteen and older put in each week.

Sean dusted his hands slowly. "I believe you. As for King Skate, here . . ."

Zach's wide-set brown eyes were innocent. "No problem. Trust me!"

"I just realized, you never did *tell* me you were free—"

"As good as!" Zach spread his hands. "School thinks I was sent to the Greendomes, the Greeners think I had to go to the Med Center, and if anyone checks that far, the Med Center will give them a 'sent home' message. This isn't just skating, this is *art*. Can't fail!"

Will tried not to laugh. Sean just looked grim.

"You said you needed as many of us as possible," Zach's joking tone turned earnest. "Philippa and Clea have morning classes and Arkady's still not back from the diving trip, so we're all you have." He grinned. "Even your dad won't blame you if I do get jugged." *Jug* was the second term Will had learned—for the additional voluntary service that the kids got assigned if they broke the rules.

At the reference to his father, who was the planetary governor, Sean flushed a little. As much as he hated being thrust into prominence by his father's position, Sean seemed to have been born with the same sense of responsibility.

As if to deny that sense, Sean gave a short laugh. "With the jug time I'm serving now for trashing that scooter during the storm, who'd notice an extra ten or twenty years?" He drummed his fingers on the bars of Zach's scooter. "I just don't want anyone looking for us. Technically we're not breaking any rules. Or weren't." He glanced at Zach, who gave his well-known lopsided grin. "I'm not driving, these scoots are legally checked out, and we're on a rock-sample expedition for geology class. The thing is, *somebody* set up that hunter's camp, unless we imagined it—"

Zach shook his head. He was still smiling, but his

eyes were serious. "Two dead and beheaded prong-horns is not my kind of daydream," he said, vividly describing his memory of the pronghorns, which were a large, herbivorous native life-form, and like all native life-forms, were protected by strict Planetary League laws. Hunting on the newly colo-nized planet carried serious penalties.

"And didn't you say that the navpak from Zach's scooter had been removed by the time the salvage team got to it?" Will asked.

Sean nodded soberly. What had been almost as strange as finding the slaughtered animals was dis-covering later that Zach's scooter had been tam-pered with so that they'd never be able to prove they'd been at the site. "Sure makes one think that somebody didn't want any coordinates on the iner-tial recorder looked at, doesn't it? So somebody might not like our nosing around that area again." He turned and climbed back on behind Zach. "Let's go."

Zach's engine whined as the pressor beam lifted the scooter a few centimeters from the road. Will felt the slight drag on his insides as his scooter lifter, then once again they raced up the road.

They're on their way, Arkady Davidov thought sud-denly, as he looked out across the sparkling blue ocean waves. *How do I know that?* As if he'd received some kind of mental transmission, the Kartai Sea before him was replaced by an image of Sean, Will and Zach racing toward the foothills of the Catalans. The image only lasted for an instant, then he was staring down into dark blue waters again.

Arkady blinked and looked around. The other

scuba students were talking and laughing, tired and exhilarated after their first expedition out to sea. Arkady leaned against the rail of the hovercraft as it moved smoothly and swiftly over the water. He stared down at the phosphorescent water, reflecting on the strange, fascinating undersea world. He'd signed up for the scuba class on discovering (after one of Zach's seemingly crazy dares) that the ocean was fun to swim in. Arkady had lived for sixteen years on Theta, a harsh, oceanless planet with very heavy gravity. His first sight of the vast stretch of the Kartai Sea had been awesome and a little frightening, but he'd swiftly become fascinated by it.

This scuba trip was something he'd looked forward to as a chance for recreation and exploration; he'd ended up swimming away from the others and searching methodically for the remains of the hoverscooter that Sean had smashed during the ion storm two months ago. In their last glimpse of it, the scooter had washed out to sea.

He couldn't quite believe it, but this morning, on their last dive, he'd found it. Arkady had grown up helping his father repair robots and vehicles, and so it was only a matter of moments before he'd gotten the navpak off. As soon as he'd reached the boat, he'd requested a short call on the community net, and during the course of an innocent conversation about school and diving, he gave a very alert Sean the last recorded coordinates on the intact inertial recorder.

Arkady's eyes squinted northward against the bright morning sun. *I wish I was with them, but Sean did not want to wait.*

Arkady couldn't blame him. Too many unsolved

questions faced Arkady and his five friends. That camp: Had Sean and Zach really seen it? None of the school or community authorities had believed them; there was no record or proof. And their being led to the site by a pack of the wild reptilian creatures called theskies had come right in the middle of that weird week of ion storms that had caused half of Ambora's colonists to hallucinate.

Sometimes even they had trouble believing they'd found the site—but then it was the *second* strange thing that they'd seen. The first, some months before, had been much stranger.

Arkady ran a hand through his short, sandy hair, remembering how he, Sean, Zach, Will, Clea, and Philippa (half of them new arrivals—and none of them well acquainted) had been sent into the Catalan Mountains as part of an emergency team installing earthquake energy displacement devices in a fault line. The six of them had wound up separated from the others. Then, drawn by a mysterious call, and accompanied by two persistent theskies, they'd been led to an isolated plateau.

Arkady still felt a chill run through him whenever he thought about what had happened on the plateau. They'd found a long-hidden device that had revealed a vision of a once-thriving city and its eventual downfall. They'd witnessed the end of a civilization, and had left the plateau dazed and grieving. They almost hadn't left at all—moments after the vision ended, a massive quake hit, destroying the remains of the city and nearly taking them with it. It was the first time since coming to Gauguin that Arkady nearly lost his life. Later, when they tried to report what they'd seen, the authorities in Ambora dismissed their story as a mass hallucination brought on by the stress. Arkady still didn't know what to make of it, though he was sure it was more than a hallucination. He shrugged, telling himself that perhaps whatever caused the vision didn't matter. What mattered was that somehow it had forged a strange, unbreakable bond among the six teens.

As the hovercraft skimmed lightly over the water, Arkady's gaze was drawn by movement along the cliff tops. He saw a dozen or so theskies silhouetted against the blue morning sun. Their triangular heads, clawed forelimbs, and long reptilian tails accented the alien quality of this seeming paradise of a world.

Squawking happily, the theskies scrambled down the pathway to the newly built dock. Now their bright orange eyes and buff-colored, feathery scales could be seen clearly.

"Oh! There's Theskie von Klausewitz!" A girl near Arkady laughed as their boat docked.

The creatures swarmed up onto the boat. *"Ackle! Ghack!"* Their raucous voices shouted a jumble of words; parrotlike, the theskies could memorize and speak words and phrases, but the scientists who had tested the creatures decreed they were about as smart as parrots.

Despite their sharp claws and long teeth, the theskies were friendly, curious, and harmless to humans. They and the quufers, the faceless little creatures that looked like hairy pillows on short legs, were to be found all over Ambora. Many of the colonists had adopted them as pets.

Theskies, Arkady thought as he reached for his gear. *Those two we called Spike and Matilda led us to the plateau, and more theskies led Sean and the others to the camp. But supposedly these creatures aren't intelligent.* He shrugged, ending up with the same conclusion he'd already come to a dozen times: *There's a lot about this planet we still don't know.*

"Well, we're here, according to those coordinates Arkady gave you," Zach said, looking around. "Sure you didn't get 'em backwards?"

Sean jumped off the back of the scooter. "Looks like any other clearing, doesn't it?" He shook his head. "Tell you what. Let's you and I collect rock samples to make Dr. Kovitch happy, and let Will do his magic to prove our sanity."

Will felt his neck getting hot. He made a business of shutting down his scooter and picking up his pack, avoiding looking at the others with what he knew was a red face. *Most of the time I feel completely useless, but as soon as someone mentions one of the few things I'm good at, I feel like an idiot.*

Zach gave him a quick smile that could have been sympathy, then he pointed at some quartz gleaming in the sun a few meters away. Sean and Zach wandered off, leaving Will alone in the clearing.

Will breathed slowly, shoving thoughts about the camp, danger, school, and his own weakness from his mind. His father had taught him the Whitehorse family traditions, though it had been two generations since anyone in the family had been back to Earth and the old Amerind territory. Will allowed his senses to gauge his surroundings. Sight . . . sound . . . smell. He moved, for once forgetting his clumsiness; his footsteps were soundless. *Touch . . .*

Arkady went home to dump his gear, clean up, and change. There was still a little time before midshift; maybe he could get in a workout at the gym before he had to go to school. Arkady's stocky body was well developed from his years on Theta. He was probably the strongest kid in the entire school, and though he now lived in what felt like low gravity, he worked out often to keep his muscle tone.

Maybe he'd see the girls—and as he thought that, he felt that strange mental tug. *Philippa. In Oblitt's history class right now, pretending to pay attention . . .*

The vivid image dissolved, leaving Arkady with a faint sense of vertigo.

Someday somebody's got to explain that.

"This branch here had something heavy hanging from it for quite some time," Will said and pointed upward. "See where the bark is worn? And look at the weeds directly beneath: there's a slightly different pigmentation here—"

"Caused by the pronghorn's blood soaking into the ground?" Zach asked grimly, his usually friendly face looking sickened.

Will nodded. "Then over here, something heavy was parked—the grass has grown back in at a uniform length."

Sean had been looking around. "Now I remember this place," he said. "This is the spot all right."

"So we tell Dr. Ives again?" Zach asked unenthusiastically.

Sean shook his head slowly. "Let's tell Arkady and Clea and Philippa. We already know that we need proof—concrete, and lots of it—to convince anybody in charge. A worn branch and those

weeds won't go far with Santori. He'd have to see a
map and a model first, and even then . . ."

Both Will and Zach grimaced at the thought of
the sarcastic assistant director. Bradbury's princi-
pal, Dr. Ives, called Laser Eyes by the students, was
formidable, but Will had to admit the guy was fair.
At least he listened. His assistant, Mr. Santori,
seemed to assume from the start that anything that
didn't follow his school rules was a scam, and he
was very fluent about expressing his disbelief.

"A model . . ." Sean looked up and grinned suddenly. "That's it. Will! Think Paul'd loan us his lab?
We'll need the big program."

At the thought of his fourteen-year-old genius
stepbrother, Paul Riedel, Will repressed a sigh. It
wasn't that Paul was particularly awful, he was
just—a genius. "He might," he said slowly.

"We need a model? Of what?" Zach put in.
"Camp? Rocks? Theskies?"

"None of 'em." Sean switched to a tone that mim-
icked his father's political proclamations. "We shall
make a holographic model of our city." He jerked
his thumb at the scooters. "Mount up! Let's ride."

"Does he make sense to you?" Zach asked Will
with exaggerated concern as they guided the scooters down the slope.

Will laughed, but before he could speak, Sean
swatted Zach on the shoulder. "Home, driver! Or
we're gonna be late."

TWO

Bad News

Zach and Will drove straight to Transport, where Zach checked in his borrowed hoverscooter. Midshift was minutes away. As the two boys watched Sean head toward the huge Education Dome that housed Bradbury School, Zach turned to Will, wondering how to word his request.

To his surprise, he saw Will's wide face split by a knowing grin. "Run you home?" Will asked.

Relieved, Zach nodded.

Will drove Zach out to Admin Hill, where most of the colony's Planning Committee was located. The Yamoto family rated space among these spacious domes partly because of the size of their family— seven kids and two adults—and partly because Zach's father, as a retired Commander in the Planetary League Space Force, now ran the planet's Communications Department.

They reached the hill at the midshift changeover.

11

Will said quickly, "See you later," and headed back toward city center.

Zach toggled the door open to his family's dome, listening cautiously. For once the place was quiet— all seven kids, two parents, and the myriad neighbors, friends, theskies, and quufers that seemed to hang around all the time were elsewhere.

Breathing a sigh of relief, Zach headed for the kitchen—and was surprised by a pleasant non-human voice. "Who has come home? I have a message for—"

A silver robot glided in, a loco, which was the colonists' term for the guardian robots, or INtegrated LOcal COntrol PARENTal Information Systems. Zach looked up calmly and said, "Off with his head!"

The loco promptly went into its inactive mode. Zach stepped up and fiddled with its programming keys. The locos were used as babysitters in most families, and outsmarting them was something the older kids put a great deal of time into. "There," Zach said at last. "Loco no see Zach, no report Zach." He sent the loco away, and retreated to his room.

He'd just started up one of his favorite vids when the door cycled open and his next youngest brother Tris bounded in. "Got ya!" Tris's wide-set brown eyes gleamed with triumph. His face changed to interest as he looked into the vidtank. "What's this? Those old ships—hey! That's *swordfighting*!" Tris's skinny body blocked the tank from Zach's view as he waved an imaginary sword around. Then his expression turned sour. "I'm *glad* you got caught. Not fair, you getting away with skating school to watch a vid—"

"It's research," Zach said loftily. "That's Rafael Sabbatini's *Captain Blood*. A classic ancient vid from the flatscreen days."

"Research? For what?" Tris squawked.

"Uh, making a vid. History-class project," Zach invented rapidly.

Tris gazed at his brother in admiration. "You mean, having fun swordfighting, and taping it, and getting *school credit*? What a hyborious scam!"

Zach shrugged modestly, glad that Tris wasn't asking any more questions about the morning.

"When are you going to—oh! Forgot!" Tris poked him. "Mom sent me because you can't turn me off, she said. Did you fix the loco again? Anyway, you're to come to Med-Peds right now. Take me to school, and leave the craft for Mom."

Medical Pediatrics was where Dr. Jacinta Yamoto worked. "Mom wants me?" Zach groaned.

"Probably wants to yell at you before you get jugged by Laser Eyes." Tris said cheerfully. "What's this, the fourth time you've gotten nabbed skating school this rotation? Fifth?"

Zach got up reluctantly. "Mom's getting too good at debugging loco scams," he said. "Let's go."

"She put the hovercraft on auto to send me home," Tris said in disgust. "How about letting me drive to school?"

Zach shook his head firmly. "If—*when*—you crash it, I'd be jugged till I'm ninety."

"Toroid," Tris muttered. "How's a guy expected to become a great stunt driver if no one lets him do it?"

Arkady emerged from the gym at midshift. He had a study period scheduled before his first class, and though he'd finished all his homework before leaving on the scuba trip, he wandered in the direction of the Information Resource Center at the midshift bell.

The girls are there—Philippa's there, he thought with sudden certainty. Was he right, or was his imagination providing these images? No, it was definitely not his imagination; all six of them had felt this mental current ever since the night on the plateau.

Why not test it? He made his way up to the balcony that ran around the main floor of the IRC. Turning his back to the neat stacks of dataspools, he looked out over the study carrels below.

Almost at once he saw them. Clea's long, shiny dark hair hid her topaz eyes as she bent over her work intently. Next to her, at another terminal, Philippa was typing in a code. Arkady looked down at Philippa, whose snow-colored cloud of hair and light-colored skin stood out startlingly from the browner skin and hair of the colonists around her. Another person that pale might be regarded as a freak; Philippa's features were so beautiful she might, had she been less standoffish, have been the most popular girl in the school.

Philippa's perfect face was serious, her sapphire eyes intent on the terminal. On first meeting her, Arkady had assumed like everyone else that the polite distance she maintained between herself and the rest of the population stemmed from the fact that she came from the governing class of Alphorion, Earth's oldest colony planet. Alphorion was considered the most highly cultured of the planets; all other worlds seemed crude in comparison. Here, on Gauguin, both of Philippa's parents were on the Gauguin's elite Planning Committee. Arkady found her attractive despite the touch-me-not attitude—not that Philippa had noticed. When she dated, it seemed only Sean Matthews was suitable.

She's certainly ignored me since that night when we were trapped on the cliff, Arkady thought. That night, during the ion storm, Arkady had seen a different side to Philippa; faced with impending death, they had talked about home, and regrets. Arkady had mentioned Anna, the girl he'd left behind on Theta. What Philippa talked about had taken Arkady completely by surprise. She'd confessed that she'd been arrested for involvement with Alphorionite revolutionaries, and that she and her family had been disgraced. *Does she regret those few words? he wondered. Does she think I'll spread it around—*

Arkady's thoughts were suspended when he saw Philippa's smooth, pale brow crease faintly. She flicked a look sideways, as if to ascertain that Clea was busy, then her fingers tapped swiftly on the console.

A moment later Philippa's body went rigid and her eyes stared, widened, at the screen.

Zach pulled onto the wide parking flat. It was easier to find a spot this late in the day, on this side of the Medical Dome. He guided the hovercraft into the Yamoto parking spot, and winced as the Med Dome's doors hissed open. As always, he was hit by that horrible smell: a combination of cleaning fluid, lab chemicals, and heavily recycled air. With a mother who worked as a pediatrician, he was very familiar with that smell, and he had decided a long time ago that he preferred to avoid it.

He took the elevator down to Pediatrics. Inside the waiting room, small children played with the toys or climbed on the carpeted squares in the far corner. In the partitioned-off annex, he saw two parents waiting with sick kids. A father and a mother each sat with a small blanket-wrapped bundle on their laps. The parents' faces wore that familiar look of controlled worry, and the kids gazed miserably into space. Zach turned to the reception intern.

"May I help—oh. Zach Yamoto?" The young man clearly recognized Zach.

Zach nodded, fighting the urge to scowl. Wasn't the guy's fault that Zach looked like his mother. Not that he really minded looking like his mother. This place was getting to him.

"You know the way?" Seeing Zach's nod, he added, "Go right in."

Zach strode down the hallway to his mother's office cubicle. The room was crowded with stored data spools, bound printouts, toys, medical equipment, and on one wall she had managed to clear enough space to hang a large framed flatpic of Galahad, her home planet, taken from space. The planet looked like a huge pearl suspended against velvet, and most of her young patients responded to its beauty.

His mother stood, absorbed in reading a chart as it printed out.

She looked up immediately, brushing her hair back with the same gesture that all seven of her children used. "Zach."

"Ma." Zach kissed her. "What is this? I'm going to

get a lecture from old Laser Eyes at school before he sends me to fertilize plants or shovel sand, and I'll probably get one from Grumps in the Greendome as well. I hope you didn't yank me in just for a third."

His mother carefully cut the flimsies from the now-silent printer. "You look tired," Zach added without thinking.

She glanced up, eyes crinkled humorously. "No lecture from me, Zach, though what Dr. Ives or the Greendome Supervisor might say to you is up to them. You know you did wrong, and I know you know. I also know that you're ahead of your group in astrophysics, which might have had something to do with your reasons for cutting."

She gestured toward a chair. Zach dropped into it. "And so?"

His mother grinned. "You haven't guessed yet? And I thought you could scent a scam a light-year off. You've been assigned to do your additional community service time with me."

Arkady watched Philippa sit there for several long, agonizing heartbeats. She did not move. She did not even seem to breathe.

Instinct prompted him to go and offer help. He started moving along the balcony, dodging around the crowd of students.

Below, he glimpsed Philippa leaning toward Clea, who had become absorbed in her work. Clea looked up, surprised. Philippa's head was bent, her hair hiding her expression as she talked. Clea blinked, looking concerned. She asked something. Philippa shook her head. Clea shrugged, smiled, and Philippa lifted a hand in a gesture of farewell and walked out.

Arkady reached the stairs—and met a group of older students coming up. He had to wait while they ambled past. When he got down the stairs by skipping threes, he almost lost sight of her on the crowded main floor.

Hastily, he pushed past people and saw her choose an up-escalator. What was wrong? By now he was desperate to stop her, talk to her, find out what had happened.

Zach fidgeted with a pile of folders on his mother's desk.

His mother was watching him with concern. He certainly did not appear to be relieved at her big news. They both lifted hands to brush hair away from their eyes. Both saw the other using the identical nervous gesture, then laughed suddenly.

Zach's laugh sounded strangled, and he saw her face settle into its professionally calm expression. "What's wrong, Zacho?" she asked.

Zach sighed. "I know I'll sound like a real vacuum-skull, but I think I'd just as soon do the usual jug-type work. Like shovel sand."

"The choice isn't yours to make," his mother replied. "Apparently they've got a full complement of victims at the Greendome and so forth. What's the problem here?"

Zach grimaced. His fingers jerked at the files and nearly sent them spilling. His mother's hands swooped, righting the pile, then her fingers closed around his hand. "Tell me, Zach!"

Zach stared at his mother's hand on his. She hadn't held his hand since . . . well, he couldn't remember when it was, but he *did* remember pushing hers away because some other boys who were playing nearby might see. He stared at her fingers. They used to seem so long and strong, and now they were like a little kid's. His own hand was much larger than hers. He looked up and shrugged. "All right. I'll try: It stinks here."

"Stinks?" A soft laugh escaped her. "How?"

"I don't know . . . but if I came in blindfolded, I'd know where I was in a second. It's always been that way. Maybe I'm just squeamish."

"My son, who likes the idea of riding twenty-meter waves, squeamish? Tell me exactly what you smell."

Zach sighed. "That cleaning fluid for one thing—"

"Which is exactly the same stuff used at the school. And the Research Dome. I notice it first thing if I go over there early in the morning. What else?"

He shrugged uncomfortably. "Chemicals . . . lab smells . . ."

She let go of his hand and stood up. "Come with me."

"Hey, Arkady! I've got to tell you about—" Will Mornette appeared out of the crowd.

"In a tenner," Arkady called over his shoulder.

He dashed up the escalator in time to see Philippa disappear through the door to the parking decks. She was moving fast like someone in a nightmare.

Arkady followed her to the entrance to the parking deck where he saw her look about quickly, then climb into the seat of a hovercraft. Within seconds, the craft rose on its pressor beam; Arkady set off after her, but before he'd covered half the lot, Philippa had deftly turned about and raced down the ramp. He slowed to a stop. Looking down at the name on the parking space, he saw *Yamoto*.

Raising his eyes, he caught the gleam of sunlight on the vehicle's bubble as it sped away up the main road. Arkady stood silently, trying to comprehend the fact that Philippa Bidding had just stolen the Yamoto family's hovercraft.

Zach followed his mother silently. They walked down two long halls. Closed doors lined either side. She stopped before the last door and laid her hand on it. Then she took Zach's hand and laid it next to hers on the door. He watched, puzzled.

She said, "Shut your eyes. Concentrate. Tell me what you smell."

Zach shut his eyes, feeling stupid. He sniffed cautiously, trying to identify—anything. There wasn't any smell. He tried a long sniff, and—there it was again.

"What's *in* there?" He yanked his hand away from the door. His mother put her finger to her lips warningly as she led him away.

"That is another door to the reception area. On the other side are toys, furniture—and sick babies and worried parents."

"What?" Zach muttered. "This doesn't make any sense."

As soon as they were back in her office, his mother put her hands on his shoulders. "I hate to be the one to tell you, my boy, but your problem isn't an oversensitive nose, it's oversensitive antennae."

"Huh?" Zach wiped his clammy hands on his pants.

"You've hid it well, Zacho." She chuckled. "But the truth is out. The 'smell' isn't a smell at all. What you are sensing when you walk into this place is fear, anticipation and the mental malaise that goes with illness. You've associated these with the air here. They make you feel bad because you think you can do nothing about them."

Zach shrugged. "Still not tracking, Ma."

"In a word, then: You're an empath."

Zach's jaw dropped.

"Come on!" She laughed. "Let's see how strong you are and get you started on doing something about it."

THREE

A Blast from the Past

The cold wind from the vent blew directly onto Philippa's face.

The hovercraft had been warmed by the sun when she first climbed into it. As soon as she left the parking deck, she opened the vents, and then turned to disengage the inertial recorder. When she arrived back in Ambora, she would reset it again, along with the clock. This way no one would know where the craft had been.

She had not practiced this kind of highly illegal trick for a long time, but her fingers remembered the job well, and now, as they had the first time or two on Alphorion, they trembled just a little as they moved along the wires.

When she was done, she set a course for Gandria, the planet's smaller second city, high in the Catalan Mountains. She no longer felt hot and sweaty—if anything, the air inside the bubble was chilly—but she did not turn the vent down. The stream of cold air on her face somehow felt cleansing.

She'd never thought to see the Leffie secret message code again, especially not tagged to her name when she logged onto the computer to begin her homework. The message had not been complicated.

I'm here in Gandria. Usual place. Come now. M.A.

M.A.—Miguel Arcaro.

Philippa stared back into memory. Two years ago—on Alphorion. She saw Miguel's serious eyes framed by the long lashes she had always wanted to touch and never had dared to. Miguel's fine, patrician features; the way his lips curved when he spoke about the thing that mattered to him most.

Philippa rubbed her own eyes. The image would not go away.

Remembering Miguel made all the old pain and disgrace come flooding back. Philippa's eyes blurred suddenly. She leaned forward and slapped the auto-pilot key. It was time to face those old memories, because she was about to meet the cause face to face.

Zach groaned. "Ma, if that's a joke, I'm not laughing."

Dr. Yamoto pointed to her picture of her home planet, Galahad. "You already know that a lot of us who are second- and third-generation Galahadans are born with empathic abilities—"

"But I was born on Earth!"

"Whatever it was that got into our genes seems to appear in some of our offspring. Not all." Zach's mother grinned suddenly. "I don't think there's any mystery about your brothers. But I'd wondered about you—and I think your sister Portia is going to have to be tested soon."

Zach sighed. "So what now? My jug's going to be psi tests? More labs and smells?"

His mother laughed. "Your jug is going to consist of learning how to block empathic awarenesses when you don't want them. We call this 'shielding.' Then I'll teach you how to use it, called 'focusing,' when you do. Then we'll see." She opened the door. "Now come into this room and watch this vintage training vid from my old home on Galahad. . . ."

Philippa had found it so easy to join the separationist movement. *Les Enfants de la Liberté*: Miguel, the leader, always used the full name instead of the nickname "Leffies." He felt that the symbolism of the name (the descendants of the Earthers, and the older meaning that had to do with one of the first successful democratic revolutions on Earth, Philippa had not been quite sure which) had been perfect. Miguel was totally devoted to the movement. He truly believed that Alphorion was *better* than Earth, and that it should be able to govern itself. The Earth-based Planetary League had no real interest, beyond trade, in the colony planets any more than Alphorion had an interest in Earth.

Well, Philippa had been fourteen, and she admitted now that she was more thrilled by the idea of secret meetings, and by being close to Miguel— winning his rare smile—than she was by the preaching of the senior members. Besides, even at age fourteen, she was already tired of being regarded by both boys and girls as a brainless fool with a holovid actress figure.

Miguel had recruited her to act as a courier, running messages—usually changes in the communication codes—by hand to various drop-off points. It was exciting to move among the tall, elaborate buildings and sophisticated crowds of the capital city, knowing that most people saw a dumb kid while actually she was carrying forbidden secrets for her hard-working allies.

"It was worth it," she muttered, staring out at the dramatic cliffs and rocky inclines of the mountains below Gandria. "Alphorion *should* be self-governing." Not that she had let herself think much about the Leffies and their plans since she had lifted ship from Alphorion. Thinking about it brought back the reasons she and her parents had had to leave. "What was stupid was me getting mad at Miguel, and then getting myself caught."

She shook her head, but the old memories would not go away. Here she was, running swiftly toward—who knows what . . . .

"To Miguel," she said his name softly. And noticed that the lump of pain inside had changed. "Miguel," she said again.

Thoughts of Sean Matthews, whom she'd dated occasionally since her arrival on Gauguin, now had as much substance as the patches of fog drifting down the high mountains. To see Miguel again—that was why she grabbed the hovercraft and was racing high into the mountains. It had nothing to do with the Leffies.

"Except," she said as the hovercraft topped a rise and she caught a distant gleam of sunset on the domes of Gandria, "Miguel *means* Leffies."

That was what had caused that last horrible argument. Philippa remembered the meeting breaking up. Miguel had given her an absent minded good-bye before starting to walk off with another Leffie. Philippa had interrupted them, demanding to talk to him—demanding attention, she realized now. She accused him of all kinds of things, but basically her anger was caused by his having made clear that she was of far less importance to him than the movement. His perplexed agreement, without understanding why she should be angry, during that last, furtive, whispered interview had caused her to storm off. Her anger had increased as she began her rounds.

It figured that that was the one time she'd be followed by one of the Planetary League's Peacekeepers, and it figured she was too mad to look for any tails. Of course, she finally did register the two Peacekeeper hovercraft flanking her when she parked outside her first stop, and she did manage to stuff her flimsies into a public waste obliette before the Peacekeepers caught up with her. Maybe another girl would have begun crying, saying she didn't know what the flimsies were for, since she'd only done a message-drop to help a boyfriend, and then would have given names and addresses of that boyfriend and his friends. Later Philippa wondered if that was what her parents would have preferred.

Instead, Philippa had destroyed the flimsies. This action made it clear she knew she was guilty. She also refused to give any names of co-conspirators, even after three weeks of unpleasant questioning. She insisted she'd been hired over the comm-link, had heard only code names. At the end she did cry and give them a list of code names, but those were fake ones. And, she smiled faintly now, she rather suspected that the youth counsellor who wrote them down had known it as well, judging from the sour look on her face as she wrote.

What happened afterward was the worst of all. Alphorion's planetary capital was wealthy, sophisticated, and its people were very conscious of status. Philippa's parents had held high posts in the government, and Philippa had earned a place, despite very tough competition, in the top-ranking Alphorion Capital Academy. After her arrest, though, when she returned home *no one* called or came to visit. She was told that her place in the academy had been rescinded. Then her parents had been informed that, should they wish to transfer to a new world, their fine record would guarantee their being considered first.

Philippa remembered too clearly her mother's cold green eyes in their one talk. "Quite a *coup*, Philippa! With one stupid act, you've not only finished any chance you might have had to make a future for yourself, you've also destroyed ours. I hope you'll enjoy this outworld post we're being shipped to. One of us should."

Following that were long weeks alone in her room, carrying on her studies just to pass the time until the scheduled lift-off to Gauguin.

Then there had been the day they landed. After emerging from the Spaceport Complex, Philippa's father sat silently during the short ride across the grassy river valley that was in the process of becoming the new city of Ambora. He looked around at the oddly shaped, low silanna-walled domes that were to serve as houses, and at the half-constructed roads. Philippa found out later that most people thought the strange, almost translucent silanna was pretty, but since the Biddings were accustomed to the ice-white marble, carving, and mosaics of their home world, the silanna appeared primitive. It was clear that her parents felt only disdain for the new city on this odd, blue-tinged frontier world.

As they reached the dome the Biddings had been assigned to, her father turned to Philippa and said, "Do you think you can manage to stay out of prison *here*?" Then he went inside to inspect the dome.

When she had left Alphorion, Philippa had promised herself that she'd forget the past and make the best of this new life in a new place. Here on Gauguin she strove to become the best student in the school. She *would* make a future—just see if she wouldn't.

But now, today, trillions of miles and over a year after she'd seen him last, came this message from Miguel. What did he want? She'd had no contact with him after she'd been arrested. Had he found out about the arrest? Of course he must have. What had he been told?

Philippa put her hands down, staring ahead at the approaching city. She realized it didn't really matter what he'd been told. What mattered now was that he wanted to see her. This meant that, after all, she had another chance. Proving herself to her parents was a lost hope—they'd never notice if she jumped off a volcano—but now she had a chance to prove herself to Miguel.

And maybe to herself.

When Zach emerged into the rosy glow of the long Gauguin sunset, he found Arkady, waiting. Zach's mind felt strange after the workout from those mental exercises his mother had taught him, and at first he did not question the appearance of a friend standing near the Med Dome entrance.

Then Zach saw Arkady's face as the Thetan gave him a quiet greeting. Zach felt his own problems fade as he looked into the light, cool eyes studying him so intently.

"Okay," Zach admitted. "I got nabbed skating. But no one knows where I really went—our secret trip's still a secret."

"I'm afraid there is a new problem, and I do not yet know what." Arkady spoke softly, casting a quick look over his shoulder at a pair of med-techs who came walking out the door.

"That sounds properly mysterious." Zach began with a grin, waving a hand at the parking place. "Can I give you a lift? We can talk in the—" He stopped. "The craft," he said blankly. "It's gone. Maybe my dad—"

Arkady was shaking his head. "That's what I need to talk to you about," Arkady said.

Zach thrust his hand through his hair. "Why do I get the feeling that this is going to be a very long day?"

Philippa felt her stomach tightening as she glided smoothly down the road into the mountain city of Gandria.

At the outskirts, she switched to manual. She drove into the city center, heading for the dome that housed Gandria's Information Resource Center. IRCs had been the "usual place" back on Alphorion: The younger Leffies in her group had felt that the safest place to meet was the most public spot possible. Who would be suspicious of kids meeting at the study annex?

Philippa drove up onto the wide platform next to the Administration, Education, and Recreation Dome, then parked carefully. As she shut down the power, she realized for the first time that what she had done was a crime. Stealing—so rare in Ambora—carried a stiff penalty.

"This is redeeming myself?" she muttered. *Worry about it later. Miguel's waiting.*

She walked inside as if she had important—and legal—business to do.

The dome seemed larger, more crowded and confusing than any in Ambora, as it housed several departments. There were a few long minutes of harried walking and escalator-riding as she thought: *How old is the message? Has he gotten tired of waiting and left? What if this is some kind of horrible trick?*

Her mind chattered on with disastrous questions until she saw the blue sign indicating the entrance to the IRC.

Below it, lounging gracefully and drinking a soft drink as if he had not a care in the world, was a familiar dark-haired figure. Her heart contracted at the sight of Miguel.

She hurried forward, and he looked up. There was a moment of shock when she met unfamiliar dark eyes, until she realized *of course*, he would get contact lenses. Now she gazed at him, unable to read any expression in these dark brown eyes so different from the beautiful leaf-green ones she remembered.

He'd grown. He towered over her. She whispered, "Hi, Miguel."

"Hi, Philippa," he replied. His voice was deeper.

Somewhat awkwardly, she repeated the old code to indicate that she'd received his message: "I brought the bio tape."

He nodded. His eyes were steady on hers, but the dark lenses masked any smile in them, any real emotion. Then he spoke softly, intimately. "I need your help, Philippa. I need a place to hide."

FOUR

Sunset Dancer

Sean Matthews stood at the window and frowned at the late-afternoon fog drifting over the ocean. His father, as governor and chief architect of the new colony, rated a prime location for their home. The view over Sanjo Bay from this window was spectacular, but Sean was not interested in the visual beauty. He was watching the fog creep in, and wondering where the others were.

At midshift, he'd sent a message to the other five, suggesting they meet and discuss the morning's expedition and his new idea. By the time he finished his late-shift drudge, only Will and Clea had responded. They were probably waiting now at the Greendome snack outlet near school, which was their favorite place to meet. Sean, worried about getting no response from Philippa, Zach, or Arkady, did not want to leave for the eaterie until he'd located at least one of them.

He turned to look at the chrono. Nearly 1700. He shut his eyes, thinking about the other three. *They're all moving.* Feeling a faint sense of vertigo, he banished the image quickly. *Let's just try on the comm-link, shall we?*

He punched Arkady's number—no response. What was going on? He punched the door, wishing he could go out and look for his friends.

Unfortunately, Sean's father had felt that an example must be set after the investigation of the wrecked scooter. On top of the long hours of jug time Mr. Santori, the assistant director, had dealt out, the governor took away Sean's personal driving privileges until the next ship of colonists was due to land. For Sean, this was the worst. Not being believed by the authorities was nothing unusual anymore; the extra jug time at the small-craft repair yard was actually fun, as he loved tinkering with machines (preferably fast machines), but not to drive?

Muttering under his breath, he turned to give the comm-link another try. He'd skip the Yamoto house, which was always about as crowded and organized as the Brasil Spaceport Lobby back on Earth, and try the Davidov home again.

As he crossed the room, a theskie ducked out from under a side table. The creature's bright eyes winked rapidly. "Laze-off! Laze-off Zach-off!" It chattered with its sharp white teeth flashing. "Missing hoff! Zoff!"

Sean grimaced, half amused and half annoyed. He had not noticed the theskie burrowing about in the storage area beyond the table. "Here, Cat! How'd you get in here? Let's call Arkady, huh?"

Sean knew the theskie did not really understand him, but it was something to talk to.

"Arkady-arkady-arkady," the theskie repeated, twitching its long tail. Sean reached to pat a hand over the feathery scales covering the theskie's small head.

Sean paused as the lights on the console changed, indicating that someone had arrived outside the Matthews' dome. Sean hit a key and the front door slid aside noiselessly.

"Hey there," Zach greeted him.

Arkady said quietly, "Unexpected problem."

"I called in a message for you at my place," Zach added, following Arkady in. "Didn't you try there?"

"I tried."

Sean's ironic tone made Zach laugh. "Got one of the critters, eh?"

Sean knew that Zach called his many younger siblings "critters," but he said, "Maybe it *was* a theskie, answering the comm-link. Made as much sense as one, anyway."

"Lilith," Zach said unerringly, looking around. "Eating as she talked. Must say, this place looks mighty empty. What's missing?"

"Your mother's models," Arkady spoke. "Gone in the storm?"

The Matthews family moved often enough that they had few belongings qualifying as unnecessary luxuries, except for Alison Matthew's collection of scaled-down copies of the buildings she had designed. She had made the models herself, using materials that approximated the real thing, and they had been works of art. The night of the ion storm the thin, translucent silanna walls of the common room cracked, and a high wind swept the models off their stands, smashing them into the opposite wall.

Now Sean nodded. "Looks bare, eh?"

Zach whistled. "I'll say. Your mom punched out about it?"

"At first," Sean admitted. "She says she's grateful now, as she'd always meant to correct the mistakes. Says she'll do 'em right this time. Where've you guys been?"

"Where *haven't* we been?" Zach dropped into a seat. "Arkady borrowed his father's craft so we could pick up my dad, Tris, and the middle critters, and do half a dozen other Yamoto errands."

"What? Why?" Sean asked.

"Because," Arkady said quietly, "the Yamoto hovercraft was taken by Philippa Bidding."

Fourteen-year-old Paul Riedel shifted in his seat and began creating holomodels of little needle-nosed, intra-system assault craft on his portable terminal. This was Paul's idea of doodling.

"We've no choice," Alison Matthews was saying. "We've got to have housing waiting for the new colonists who are about to land. That's part of the contract. We now know that silanna is not perfect, but it's the best construction material we've got."

"Not to mention the cheapest and the fastest," Dr. Rilvh, the director of the building materials lab, snapped.

"There *is* a way," Paul spoke up eagerly.

Joan Bidding, director of agricultural economics, fixed her ice-green eyes on his face. "We're waiting to hear it." Her voice, as always, was soft, cool, and expressionless.

Paul hunched his shoulders. All the adults looked

at him, with expressions ranging from Dr. Rilvh's impatience to his mother's encouraging smile. "Nothing concrete," he began. "But you'll remember the night of the ion storm—"

"Your account of your clever intuition about the ionization levels is in the records," Director Bidding cut in, giving him an indulgent smile. "We've all read the report. But that does not help us now." As Paul sank down in his seat, Director Bidding studied the others around the table. "It will hurt the economy badly if we have to completely rebuild the city. It seems a great risk, depending upon silanna again."

There was a short silence. Paul stared covertly at Philippa Bidding's mother; like her daughter, she had pale skin as well as blond hair, and in the gathering gloom, the whites of her green eyes had the same odd glow, caused by a harmless parasite, which marked the eyes of all natives of Alphorion. Like her daughter, Mrs. Bidding was also strikingly beautiful. Still, she reminded Paul of ice.

"Perhaps, but we haven't any other construction materials" Paul's mother, Dr. Riedel, smiled. "Either we figure out a way to reinforce the silanna, or cover it, or alter it."

"We know the problems, and we know what we need," Dr. Rilvh put in, his bushy brows knit together. "I suggest we adjourn until one of us comes up with an alternative."

Paul sat where he was as the other adults left the room, some talking softly among themselves. His mother was listening to Dr. Rilvh; she cast Paul a questioning look over the scientist's shoulder, and Paul forced himself to grin and shrug. He already felt bad enough. Why add to it by needing comfort from his mother?

A soft voice murmured: "No one has forgotten what you did, Paul."

Paul turned to see Dr. Petrov, his mentor, leaning against the lab-console as the printer chattered softly. Paul's eyes slid to the pages of flimsy spooling out of the printer. "Dismissed, maybe," he said.

"Not even that." Dr. Petrov's good humor could be heard in his low, husky voice. "No one will forget, or dismiss, your having saved the city with your discovery. But your action is now a historical fact, which does not solve the problems we are faced with today."

"Paul?" his mother spoke from the doorway. "I've got to return to the Greendome after my checkup at the Med Center." She grinned, brushing a hand against the front of her lab coat. In about half a year's time, Paul would have a new half-brother or sister. Paul wasn't sure how he felt about that, either. "I wasn't able to find Will after school. Would you run a report to the Rec Center for me?"

"Sure," Paul said.

Dr. Petrov pulled his flimsies from the hopper and waved them at Paul. "Get your mind off silanna and back on plate tectonics, boy. I want to see your figures on that measure problem I sent you!"

"I copy," Paul forced himself to speak cheerfully, and he ran out of the Research Dome. He climbed into the battered two-seater hovercraft that he shared with his mother, Will, and Will's father, William Whitehorse Mornette. Driving away from the city center, he thought back to how great he'd felt after his discovery and solution had saved what remained of the city during that storm. For days afterward, every scientist at the Research Dome had gone out of his or her way to congratulate Paul on his fast thinking, and he had felt, at last, that he really fit in despite the fact that he was five years younger than the youngest technician there.

"Fit in," he snorted, steering onto the road that paralleled the deep Tati River. "I felt like a king. Even the kids at school stopped looking at me like I was some kind of freak—for about three days."

Paul did not notice the brilliant reds, oranges, deep blues, and purples of the long Gauguin sunset, though he drove straight west. He was thinking that, though he meant well, Dr. Petrov did not really understand what it felt like. Sure, it was an honor to sit in with the scientists, and Paul was careful not to give anyone any reason to complain about his behavior—but too often, when a lab session broke up, everyone walked off with other people and Paul was either left alone or with his mentor.

Then there was school. Well, Bradbury School was small. There were three levels: Cohort One, the primary level, Cohort Two, which the kids Paul's age were in, and Cohort Three, for the older teens. New kids learned the names of everyone else within a week—and *everyone* seemed to know by now that Paul had graduated beyond the course offerings at Bradbury. As a result, kids his age tended to treat him as if he'd grown an extra nose. True, most of them were boring anyway, but . . .

Paul steered carefully into the Rec Center parking deck. He didn't know what to do. He was sick of tagging along with the older ones, and sick of being regarded as a "PC" by the rest. He wasn't even sure what PC meant, besides "point collector," and he did not want to show his ignorance by asking. He knew it had to be nasty.

Above his head, the glowglobes suddenly went on. He shoved his hands in his pockets and moved into the deserted building. It was nearly empty; most people had gone home to eat. Soon it would fill with groups of people doing various recreational activities.

Feeling lonelier than ever, Paul wandered down a back corridor.

As he rounded a corner, he heard faint music. It was not the twenty-first-century Post-Rock, which was apparently popular again nowadays. It was some ancient-sounding music, with a rising and falling melody played by one instrument. A piano, was it called?

Paul rounded another corner and saw an open door. The music was strong now. Curious, he walked to the door and looked inside.

He saw a bare room, with all the windows open to let in the last light of the setting sun. In the middle of the room, a single figure danced. Paul stood motionless, watching the graceful dancer with magenta hair, lit by the molten sunlight like a crown of fire, until his vision began to darken on the edges and a pain squeezed his lungs.

Breathe! A dim warning went off in his head, and he sucked in a breath of air. His vision cleared immediately, but the pain increased, now squeezing his heart. He backed away, thinking hazily, *That's Daphne DeVries.* And even more hazily, *What's wrong with me?*

His brain managed to produce two hypotheses:

Either I've suffered a major cardiac arrest, or I'm in love.

"Let's see ... my mother should still be at the Greendomes, and my father is probably out at Transport," Philippa said chattily talking to herself. Her voice sounded weak to her ears, but the silent figure next to her did not react beyond a brief, distracted smile.

Miguel had not spoken during the entire return drive. He'd said before getting into the hovercraft: "There might be an extra comm device hidden. Unless there is a well-lit place to stop along the way, so we can search thoroughly, then it is best we do not talk until we know we are safe."

The drive back seemed shorter than the drive to Gandria, though it was long after dark when they rounded the last peak of the Catalan Mountains above Ambora and looked down on the lights of the city. Philippa was very aware of Miguel's tall form sitting next to her. The slightest sounds were distinct—the shifting of his clothing, the change in his breathing as he looked around. Her palms had been clammy ever since she heard herself say, "I'll hide you."

It was horrible not to be able to talk, but there had been no time to find a safe place to stop. Philippa was afraid that the Yamoto vehicle's disappearance would cause a search unless she could get it back and leave it somewhere. As she drove she tried to think of plausible stories for having taken it. Her mind seemed to blank on every excuse. Instead, her thoughts veered toward Miguel. As the craft descended into the outskirts of the city, she decided it might be best just to abandon the hovercraft. Maybe questions would die down eventually if it were found.

She approached the Biddings' dome from the back, and was relieved to see that no lights were on. As she pulled up in front of the dome, avoiding the drive, she glanced at the front of the house.

She caught her breath. There, just outlined in the soft blue-white light of the street glowglobes, were two waiting figures. They turned to face the vehicle. She recognized Arkady's light hair and Sean Matthews's body. "Friends," she whispered—but a sudden touch of cool air made her aware that Miguel had noiselessly eased the door open. He slipped into the darkness.

"See you later," his voice floated back softly.

She closed his door and shut the power down. Getting out, she walked across the immaculate lawn toward the waiting boys.

FIVE

Welcome to the Zoo

Zach Yamoto cycled open the door to his home.
Inside, he found the usual confusion of lights, noise,
and bodies. Zach moved through it slowly as if he
were alone. He still couldn't believe that studious,
quiet Philippa Bidding had taken the hovercraft.

"Zach! Zach! Lilith ate all the grapes Dad got at
the Greendome—"

"I did not! Sara came over and had some, too.
And she's trying to comb the quufers!"

"Zach, Marshall's 'grammed the loco to call me a
PC again—"

"Zach, I've got to talk to you some more about
that great idea—"

"Zach's got a lotta water, huzza! Huzza! She's in
hot water!"

Zach blinked and looked around. Seeing that he
was surrounded by eyes, human and otherwise, he

smiled. "Hey, critters! Why's this place sounding more like a henhouse than usual?"

Instant pandemonium broke out as each child tried to explain just how he or she had been wronged by the others, and the theskies (Zach distractedly counted three) added to the noise by repeating and garbling everything.

They don't know what they're saying, he thought as he moved toward the menu processor. *But I wasn't talking, was I, when I thought about Philippa being in hot water?*

Of course, one of the critters could have been saying the same thing about his youngest sister, he realized a moment later, as the argument about the missing grapes penetrated his mind. "Yo, gang," he said. "Stow it just long enough for me to get some slop cooked up. Now what haven't you wiped out our ration card on?"

He selected some food for everyone, trying to solve the quarrels of the little ones as he did. Before long the youngest ones and their visiting friends were sitting more or less quietly, eating and watching *Galaxy Patrol.* Two of the theskies were squatting in front of the bright picture as well, their unwinking eyes reflecting the colors in the tank. The third theskie had disappeared, as well as the quufers.

Zach sank down with his tray in front of him, thinking: *Did Sean and Arkady find Phillipa at home?* He got up again and went to the comm-link console. No one answered at Sean's.

Shaking his head, he sat down again. As he raised his fork, he became aware of Tris hovering on the edge of his vision.

"Zach," Tris said. "You'll include us, won't you? We want to help!"

"Help?" Zach's fingers were now rubbing his forehead. "You have a problem?" He hoped he hadn't said anything out loud about the missing hovercraft.

"No *problem*," Tris's short nose wrinkled. After all, as a man of the galaxy, he was well able to handle his own problems. "Just, I've talked it over with Mik, Jehanne, and Tank, and they're all for it."

"For? It?" Zach repeated blankly.

"Haven't you been *listening*? None of us has a pri rating to check out the equipment we'd need. But we took a vote and we'll help you with yours. We'll do any job you need! So we're ready to get started right away. Can you get the others to meet with us all?"

Zach put his fork down and rubbed his eyes with both hands. "What meeting? What's the problem?"

"No problem—the history holovid—" Tris looked at his brother's puzzled expression, and his temper exploded. "Oh, forget it! Obviously, you're too busy—too *old*—to include *us*!" Tris stomped off.

"Tris! Wait!" Zach called, just to hear the hiss of the bedroom door closing. Zach shook his head. Later he'd go find out what was troubling Tris, then he'd apologize and make things all right. Now, though, he was feeling slightly sick. Like the first time he got sunburned: too sensitive all over, and faintly achy in the temples, and just a little nauseated. *I've got to eat something*, he thought, looking down at the cooling food on his tray. *Went too long today.*

He began to fork food into his mouth rather mechanically. Behind him, the smaller kids cheered noisily as the space vessels belonging to Rotten Rupert and Jezebel, the villains of *Galaxy Patrol*, were forced dangerously close to a gas giant by the avenging heroes.

Zach scarcely heard the noise. His thoughts went to Philippa Bidding's quiet, formal house. In his mind, he could see the pale colors and exquisite furnishings. The Bidding parents called the rooms by fancy Alphorion names; Zach didn't know what they meant, but he had never felt comfortable in any of them on his single visit. Now, as he thought about Philippa's home, he sensed that Arkady, Sean, and Philippa were indeed together, but the meeting was not going well—Philippa was feeling tense and sick.

Is that why I feel so rotten? That weird current connecting the six of us, teaming up with my mother's gift of Galahadan empathy, is making me share Philippa's stomachache!

Laughing ruefully, he dumped his food into the recycler and sat down to wait.

As Philippa walked up to the house, she saw that both boys' faces were serious. Her insides tightened, but her face took on the blank, polite look that had become habit with her parents and with strangers as she stepped up to the terrace.

"Arkady saw you take the Yamoto car," Sean began bluntly.

A pang of warning knifed through her brain. "Let's go inside," she interrupted, turning to the door. Behind her, the boys were silent.

The door slid open and they walked inside. Their shoes sounded loud in the parquet entry hall. Around them, lights brightened, and the air-purifier fan that her mother had recently installed puffed cool, odorless air at their faces.

A moment later a loco glided in. "Good evening, dear Philippa," its muted, emotionless voice began.

Philippa said, *"Tais-toi!"* in a low voice, and the loco turned silently away.

Philippa led the boys into the *salon. Salon . . . was someone thinking about the way my parents refer to the parlor?* Philippa's mind went hazy, as if it was trying to be in two places at once. *Oh please, don't let that mental current thing include me now.* She tried to close her mind behind a wall.

"Philippa," Sean's voice carried just a hint of exasperation. "Is there a problem?"

"No." She realized she'd let a long silence build.

Sean's brows drew into a line of irritation, but Arkady spoke lightly, "We picked up Zach's father from Admin and took him out to the comm installation on Mount Orian, and we got Zach's other chores done."

Sean took over. "So no one besides us knows that the Yamoto craft is missing. We've only got to get it to Zach's and you're covered. Meanwhile, we've got to talk about the camp, and . . ."

Philippa felt almost dizzy with relief—a feeling that faded as she remembered Miguel. *He's out there somewhere, waiting. And I've got to get him away again before my parents come back.*

"Great," she interrupted again, with a blinding social smile. "Thanks! I really appreciate it—and I'll take the car to Zach's as soon as I—get something to eat."

"Philippa," Arkady said quietly. Her eyes went to his face, which was calm but his light blue eyes were cool and serious. "Sean, Zach, and Will found that hunters' camp this morning. We need to talk—"

Sean now interrupted, looking exasperated. "Get your dinner! And if you have any free time to discuss our problem, let us know. Let's go."

There was silence then, as Arkady waited for Philippa to say something. She just blinked at them, looking as if she scarcely heard their voices. "See you at school," he said gently, turning away.

Sean started to turn away as well, but he couldn't let it go that easily. "Any more mysterious errands that need running? We'd be happy to check out a scooter for you. Better than being the first kid to land in the slammer in case we can't—" Sean's sarcasm faded out when Philippa's cheeks went completely pale.

"I've got to get back home," Arkady said quietly. "My folks'll be wondering."

Sean turned, and nothing more was said as the boys walked outside.

They walked past the Yamoto hovercraft, which was still pinging and creaking as it cooled.

"Long drive," Sean commented.

Arkady did not answer immediately. He was recalling the night of the storm. Philippa had told him just enough about her past for him to realize that an action of hers had resulted in the family being transferred.

Is this business tonight somehow related? She hasn't told anybody else, Arkady thought to himself as he walked along silently beside Sean. *Maybe she doesn't remember telling me. Maybe she doesn't realize that her past won't matter to any of us here on Gauguin. What matters to me is, she doesn't want anyone's help. Including mine.*

* * *

Philippa heard the door hiss closed behind the boys, and she sighed in relief. Glancing at her chrono, she saw that her parents were still two hours away from arrival time.

She stood in the entryway and shut her eyes. Strange, how clearly she could *see* Sean and Arkady in her mind, walking toward Sean's house.

She rubbed her eyes furiously. *Why does that current have to pull me in now? Can the others feel me?* Again she pushed away the mental image of the boys walking away from her house, trying to close her own thoughts behind a wall. Then she dimmed the entry way lights and opened the door. She stood quietly, listening and waiting.

After a time, she heard a soft, quick step. Miguel appeared beside her. She hit the door control as he walked in; as soon as the door was shut, she activated the lights again.

"My parents aren't due for an hour, but I have to return the craft," she said.

"Who were those boys?" Miguel stared down at her without any hint of a smile. "What did you tell them?"

"Classmates. They—they said that Zach's father doesn't need the craft after all. I didn't tell them anything. I don't think they'll ask again," she added swiftly, "but if they do, I'll make up something."

Miguel sighed, leaning his head back to ease a tense neck. His eyes closed, and Philippa felt a wave of tenderness. "Do you want to step into the *bain* to take out those horrid lenses? Do they hurt?"

"They itch," he said with a slight smile. "But they've protected me this far. I'm not about to complain."

"What happened?" she asked.

He shook his head once. "What hasn't?"

"Something horrible? Or—" She saw him clearly hesitating, and she said hastily, "Look. You're hungry—at least, I am—and I haven't seen you eating, so you must be! Let me get something fast, then we'll leave. I think I know a place. At least it should be all right for a while. It's a retreat house, part of the Rec complex. I happen to know that no one is scheduled for R and R there, not until we finish the increased duties we've had since the storm. . . ." She talked on, describing the house built on the very last mountain of the long Catalan chain, just above the sea. The view was one of the most beautiful in the area, and the house had all the amenities. Visiting VIPs or administrative types who requisitioned it were allowed to use it, but now it was empty. Philippa knew this because she had done drudge as an entry assistant in Housing just a few days before. She had seen the schedules for all the government-owned recreational facilities outside the city.

As she talked, she selected foods from the menu that most resembled things they had eaten on Alphorion. During all this, Miguel stood silently, his dark-masked eyes wandering from object to object in his range of vision.

When she stopped for breath, he pointed to the hallway. "That portrait is of you, isn't it?"

Philippa glanced at the portrait, which was painted by human hands, of herself as a child, with the beautiful Alphorion sky stretching across the background. She usually walked past the picture without glancing at it. Now she felt her insides tighten as she looked at the happy child she'd been. "Yes."

"Your parents—"

"A nice reminder of what we've lost."

Miguel glanced at her quickly. Again the lenses completely covering his eyes seemed to make it impossible to read his expression. "I saw them," he said softly.

"My parents?"

"In Gandria. A few days ago."

"Yes. They go there every week or so." The preparator light blinked, and she pulled the tray out. "They didn't see you."

"No." Miguel took the plate she handed him. "Thank you."

"Let's eat in the craft. I know the coordinates, and the recorder's still disengaged."

Miguel stood quietly while she doused all the lights, opened the door, and checked outside. They got into the hovercraft quickly; she drove on manual until they were off the hill, then set a course on the auto-pilot at max speed.

They could not talk, of course. Miguel pointed to the power indicator questioningly. She showed him with her fingers that they were not going a great distance. He gave a single nod, and turned his attention to his food.

Philippa ate mechanically, not tasting anything. Outside, the darkened, scrubby hillsides spun away at rapid speed. Still, it seemed to take a long time until the blinking green light indicating *course completed* let her know that they had reached the retreat. She took control and guided the hovercraft up the last of the drive, in case they might see someone unexpectedly. When they got to the house, she saw that the power reserve was frighteningly low—

driving at max speed wasted power so quickly. She had had no choice, though.

They walked up to the house. The door slid open as they approached, and lights came on. "You'll find everything you need—" she began, but Miguel's hand closed around her arm suddenly.

"There might be a recorder device on in there," he whispered against her ear. "I'll have to check."

"Sorry." His fingers relaxed and withdrew, and she rubbed her arm, trying to still her pounding heart. Inside, her dinner felt compressed into a hard ball. "Look, Miguel, I'd better go back," she whispered. "I'll return as soon as I can."

He nodded, stepping away. She walked to the craft, then looked back: He was still standing there, watching. The light was behind him; she could not see his face. She powered up and drove away.

The drive back was increasingly unnerving as she watched the power indicator hover over, then touch, the red line.

Still, she had to stop outside the Admin Hill housing complex in order to reconnect the inertial recorder. Then she drove to the Yamoto house, which was still lit. She thought she heard faint boomings and music from the holovid screen inside as she eased the scooter up into the garage. She then cut power, and the craft settled down gently on its pads as the pressor beam dissipated. Quietly, she stepped out, checked the bubble to make certain that nothing had been dropped inside, then hooked up the power recharger.

Satisfied that all was—at last—as it should be, she was about to leave, when there was a step behind her.

She whirled and backed up.

"It's Zach," came Zach's friendly voice.

She drew in a sharp breath. "Do you *always* sneak up on people?" She was surprised to hear a quaver in her voice.

Light glowed on, and there was his lopsided smile and steady light brown eyes. His eyes changed as he looked at her, from curiosity to concern. He started to speak, but she flung up a hand.

"Don't say it." She heard the quaver again, and hardened her voice. "I won't take it again, and I'm sorry, and no matter what people think. I'm not a-a thief. I just . . ." The quaver was threatening to turn into something worse. She stopped.

Zach tipped his head toward the hovercraft. "I was just going to thank you for hooking it up to recharge." He started to turn away. "Oh." He gave her another rueful smile. "The recorder—?"

"On." She gave a ragged laugh.

"Good night," he said gently, and walked toward the house.

Philippa watched Zach go, too surprised to move. She wasn't sure what she'd expected from him, but it certainly wasn't the unquestioning acceptance he'd given. Still shaking with tension, she cut through two neighbor's gardens. At home, she saw by the lights in windows that one of her parents had arrived. No signs of alarm, though: she touched the outside override and opened the door manually, which was quieter, and slipped inside.

No one was in sight. Light and faint noise came from her parents' rooms, which were at the opposite end from her own.

She dashed into her room, ran straight through it to the *bain*, and was sick.

SIX:

Closed Circuit

"Do-dum-DO-o-h-dum. *Crack!*" Daphne DeVries sang in a mournful voice, providing the sound effect at the end of each line. She was carrying a roll of wire to the rest of her building team. After handing the wire up to Clea Tourni, Daphne lifted her low-crowned, flat-brimmed hat in order to wipe her brow on her sleeve. "Whew!"

"Why wear a black hat on a sunny day?" Clea asked, laughing.

"It's a villain hat." Daphne squinted up at Clea, who was perched on the delicate-looking framework of wires that soon would shape the walls of a dome. "I woke feeling villainous. Now, after slaving away all morning in this sun, I am reduced to a Russian serf. Do-di-Doooo-dum. *Boom!* The song was called, I wot not why, 'The Volga Boatmen.'"

"Yo! DeVries! Cut the talk and get that wiring up! This team's only on eight, and we've a quota to fill if you want to go home tonight!" Markey, the lanky, sun-bronzed construction leader called as she passed by with a loaded hoversled.

"Mercy!" Daphne croaked, pantomiming raising shackled hands.

"Here!" Clea offered, laughing. "Get ahold of the end of this wire!"

Clea was now an experienced high-wire runner. She and Daphne quickly finished the silvery network of wires, then jumped down as the rest of the team opened the containers of dry-processed silanna and plugged them into the acceptor arrays. Most of the team promptly began walking to the next dome site. Clea lingered, watching. The silanna seemed to grow miraculously, spreading in a thin, earth-toned layer over the wire framework. Soon it would cover the framework smoothly, and there would be another dome, all ready for a new family.

Clea had worked on construction detail during at least part of every rotation period since her family first arrived, but she never tired of watching the silanna walls grow. Both the beauty of the silanna and the fact that she was helping to make a home for other people gave her so much pleasure that she really never minded this job. Of course, she complained about drudge just like anyone else, and now as the whistle blew for a break, she turned away with loud expressions of relief.

Daphne had also lingered. She wound her long, magenta hair about one hand and fanned the back of her neck with her hat. "Shall we hie ourselves tenward and see what surprises await?" Daphne waived at the temporary shelter set up for sector's construction crew.

"You know what awaits." Clea wrinkled her nose. "Grumps's Gauguin Punch, and those corrosive 'highly nutritive' protein snacks!"

Daphne made a wide gesture with her hat. "Swill for the slaves!"

Clea laughed, falling in step beside her. Working with Daphne, who was a relative newcomer to Ambora, was fun. Daphne had announced soon after her arrival that she wanted to become an actress, just like her mother, who was still touring with a troupe on faraway planets. And today she made the construction time speed by with her funny stories and quotations from ancient and modern plays.

Now they entered the shelter and joined the group around the cooler. Daphne jammed her hat back on her head and began another running dialogue, this time about the very unlikely foods that might await them, when Clea's attention was drawn by a peculiar but unmistakable inner sensation. *Someone's thinking about me.*

She looked through the doorway. No one there.

"Clea?" Daphne said at her shoulder, her wide gray eyes questioning.

"Oh! Sorry. Mind must have wandered off and abandoned my brain." Clea grinned.

"Yon varlet wants to know our desires." Daphne waved her hat at the waiting teammate who was in charge of today's break rations.

"Citrus," Clea said hastily, and was tossed a container.

"Shall we remove ourselves from the milling masses?" Daphne suggested after getting her container of cold juice.

It's Zach. Searching . . .

"I—" Clea frowned, blinking. She knew now that Zach Yamoto was somewhere nearby, though as yet she had not seen him. "I'll be back in a tenner," she murmured and walked away.

Daphne stared at Clea's retreating figure, then followed reluctantly, just as far as the door of the shelter.

She was not really surprised to see Clea cross the newly paved pathway toward a hovercraft. In it, Daphne recognized Zach Yamoto's long-haired figure. A moment later, a small, fast-moving hoverscooter zoomed up and stopped perilously close to the little group. Driving it was muscular Arkady Davidov, and behind him sat Sean Matthews.

Daphne sighed, thinking wryly: *Well, they always say that eavesdroppers hear what they deserve, so I guess spies should see what they deserve.* Here she had spent a fun morning with Clea Tourni while working—but now, at the break, Clea rushes off to be with the three most attractive guys in the entire Bradbury School.

Not that it was any simple matter, such as one girl flirting with three guys. What made Daphne feel that cold stone of rejection was that she knew Clea wasn't officially dating any one of those guys. Instead, she and the three guys—plus tall, thin Will Mornette and the most beautiful girl in the school, Philippa Bidding—seemed to have formed a closed circle. Newcomers just couldn't get in.

Or, Daffy Jet-mouth DeVries can't get in, she thought, turning away abruptly. *Can't make friends last, can't make a home last.*

Delete thought! She swept off her hat, and finding the eyes of some of the teens on another work crew following her gesture, she began to intone a long poem about slavery on the spaceways.

Clea watched Arkady and Sean race up in the battered two-seater from the repair yard. "Seen Philippa?" Sean asked Clea abruptly.

"No," Clea said. "Doesn't she usually have the same drudge as you? Not to mention jug time as well?" She grinned to herself, remembering when that kind of luck had seemed unfair.

Now Sean looked seriously annoyed. "Yeah. She, Arkady, and I were supposed to spend morning jug at the repair yard today. She apparently showed just before we got there, and gave the head tech some scam about having been transferred. So she wasn't sent out here?"

"Not that I've seen," Clea said cautiously. She could feel Sean's anger now. Something more than just skating jug was wrong. "Philippa's not the kind to skate," Clea added reflectively.

Zach gave her a lopsided smile. "You know where she is right now?"

"Of course not! I just said . . ." Clea's voice trailed off.

Zach nodded. "Exactly. Where's Will?"

"He's . . . over there." Clea waved a hand in the direction of the five huge domes that comprised Ambora's city center. The tops of those domes, gleaming softly in the morning sun, were just visible to the south of them. "That's weird. How can she shut us out?"

Sean shrugged impatiently. "Since we don't know how it works that we can track each other, I think the question really is, *why* is she shutting us out? Particularly after last night."

"Last night? Did something happen?" Clea asked. "I went to bed early." She looked perplexed. "And I had bad dreams."

"At least you didn't lose your dinner, oh, about midnight," Zach said ruefully.

"This isn't helping," Sean snapped. "What's with the girl?"

Clea looked at the others. Sean's green eyes were stormy, Zach looked puzzled, and Arkady's face was sober as he studied his hands.

Zach finally shrugged. "Well, I'm overdue for my own jug—but it's with my mother, so I can be a little late. Looks like Philippa doesn't want us in on whatever she's up to."

"Then let's give her a hand and pay no attention to her whatsoever," Sean said. "That is, *if* she shows up for class this afternoon."

Behind Clea, the whistle blew again. This served to send the boys off in opposite directions. Clea walked slowly back toward the construction site. She noticed distractedly that Daphne was talking to a grinning audience of kids from a different group. Clea was relieved. She needed some time to think.

When the midday whistle blew, Daphne gave the others a general wave and set off at a brisk hike toward the Entertainment Center. Her father was the new director, and their dome was behind the complex. She would eat lunch alone, to spare herself having to ask someone for company or to be not asked by someone.

"Someone like Clea," Daphne muttered. "All right! So they think I'm a toroid. Maybe it's my glorious mane!" She shook her head, her hip-length hair blowing in the breeze. "Perhaps I should make a statement and wear only magenta clothes. No. Green!"

To cheer herself up, she began singing the lyrics from a musical. Arriving at the complex, she paused when she saw a knot of young kids standing outside her father's office.

"Hey—maybe we can ask her" the foremost kid said. She recognized his lopsided smile and wide-spaced light brown eyes; he could only be one of Zach's brothers.

"Can I help you?" She gave them a flourishing wave of her hat.

"Well, I hope so!" Tris grinned. "It's about taping equipment. Ah, handcams. And effects computers . . ."

"For recvids," one of the other kids put in.

"*And* classics," a girl cut in hastily.

"What, who, and why?" Daphne asked. "My dad will need to know!"

Tris thrust two of his friends aside. "Can you keep a secret?"

Daphne lifted her hands. "Look, I hate jug time as much as any—"

"It's not *illegal*," Tris interrupted, whispering. "It's just . . . if you can keep it a secret . . . we want to make a vid! Our *own* story, and shoot it ourselves, and we don't want anyone to know until it's done!"

"Especially know-it-all Thirds," the girl said sourly.

Daphne thought of her peers in Cohort Three at school. She laughed. "I'll keep your secret—who would I tell? Except my father, of course, but I'll let him know it's a private project. I'm sure we can get you a handcam and a bit of vidtape. You'd best plan your schedule carefully, as there isn't much vid equipment allotted yet for rec purposes! But, do any of you know how to work in the effects program? It's difficult and delicate."

The kids exchanged grimaces and shrugs.

"If you know anything about model projections, that would get you started in understanding how the effects program works," she added. "It's not easy—I'm just learning it myself!"

"We don't," Tris said. "But I think ... I know someone who might. We'll be back," he promised as he pushed his group toward the far door.

Daphne grinned. She hoped Tris and his friends would be back.

Clea plumped down in a seat, set her terminal down before her, and watched the robot tutor glide smoothly into the classroom. Behind her, Sean leaned forward and whispered, "Meet after class."

The robot tutor turned and faced them, and the sounds of whispers and terminals being set up died away. Then the door hissed open, and Philippa Bidding darted into the room. The tutor's blank face turned in her direction as she sank into a seat and slapped her terminal into operating mode.

Throughout the tutor's lecture, Clea found her eyes drawn to Philippa. The Alphorionite's skin was naturally very pale, but today it seemed to Clea that the other girl had no color in her face at all. Something was definitely wrong.

At the end of what seemed like an endless biochemistry lecture, Clea saw Zach catch Philippa's attention. The blond girl followed the other five slowly, almost reluctantly. But if she was afraid of questions, she did not get them.

The six of them moved into an alcove. "Glad you made it to class, Philippa," Sean said evenly.

Clea saw faint color enter the other girl's cheeks.

Sean went right on. "We found the camp yesterday—the one where we saw the pronghorns—"

"Speaking of which," Will put in hesitantly, "Daphne was there that first time, wasn't she? She's asked a few questions about things that happened during the storm. And about why nothing was ever done about the pronghorns."

Clea nodded. "She was a big help that week. I hate to put her off."

"We have to," Sean said. "I mean, I think we do. We were called by *some*thing to see that vision on the plateau. And ever since then, all these weird things, and some dangerous ones, have been happening to us. In fact, things keep getting weirder, and no one in authority believes us. So we need to assemble proof. And we need to find out if the vision and what's been happening—this current, for example—are all caused by the same thing. We need to identify the danger, and to gather proof of what we saw. Until we do these two things, I think we're better off keeping this to ourselves. I don't want anyone else at risk."

Clea looked around and saw assent in her friends' faces, even Philippa's tense expression.

Sean nodded. "I guess we're agreed. Now to problem one. I got an idea yesterday. I'm hoping we can get access to one of the big terminals at the Research Dome, and work on building a model of the city. Seems to me if the six of us, using our memories of that vision, can get something detailed together, we can run the result by the archeologists and see if they can identify it. Go from there."

"I'll check today with Paul about his lab," Will said.

"Then how about meeting tomorrow afternoon, when we all have free time? That all right?" Sean looked around at the others.

Clea watched Philippa nod slowly.

Daphne set her portable terminal on a shelf and punched up her practice music. She tossed her tunic next to the terminal, and eyed herself in her black tards. "Why do you keep trying?"

She had dawdled after class this afternoon, hoping maybe to get Clea to walk with her to the Greendomes for a snack. Instead, Clea had hurried after Zach and Will; a moment later, Daphne was out as well, just in time to see six heads disappear into a study alcove.

She tossed her hair back as the piano music filled the room. Her spine straightened, and she moved to the barre to begin warm-ups.

As usual, the precise concentration required for ballet soothed her mind as it exercised her body. She finished at the barre and moved out onto the floor to begin her combinations—and paused when she saw a shadow at the door.

Looking over, she saw that kid again. The short, skinny one who was apparently related in some way to Will Mornette. Hadn't he been here yesterday? She gave him a wave, and saw him duck his head and blush.

She danced across the floor again, but when the music paused, she smiled at her rapt audience. "Hi! What's your name?"

"Paul." He sounded croaky, as if he had a cold.

"If you like ballet—and so few people do—I've got some vids of *good* performers!"

"You're good," came the answer, even more hoarsely.

She laughed, shaking her head. "Try telling my old teacher that—" She stopped when she saw that the doorway was empty. *Poor kid*, she thought. *Maybe I should have offered him a ride to the Med Center.*

SEVEN:

Secret Projects

Philippa's heart was beating painfully when she arrived home from school. As soon as she stepped inside she heard the air vent go on, which told her even before the loco floated in that no one was home.

"Good afternoon, dear Philippa," came the melodious voice of the loco. "Your parents have been delayed at an administrative planning session for the incoming colonists—"

"I have to study at the IRC," Philippa said calmly. *"Tais-toi."*

The loco promptly shut down. It would reactivate as soon as someone spoke to it; should her parents arrive home first and want to know where she was, which was unlikely, the loco would tell them about the IRC.

She had eaten nothing since the night before; her head felt strangely empty, rather than her insides, but she knew she had to eat. As she waited for the preparator to finish its work, she thought rapidly.

I hope I've remembered everything. She saw a momentary image of Sean Matthews, standing at the scooter repair yard, and forced it out of her mind. She had raced straight to the yard after school, checked out a scooter for a test run, and left before any of the afternoon drudge help had time to show up.

She took a few hasty bites, then gathered her portable terminal and study spools, and left.

She drove at a moderate pace off Admin Hill. As soon as she was out of sight of the houses, she sped up.

She drove for a time, performing and logging checks of various aspects of the craft; when she reached the fork of the road that led up to the Retreat House, she stopped the scooter and disengaged the inertial recorder. She'd activate it again when she returned to this spot.

"I believe I've thought of everything," she said aloud. Her insides were beginning to cramp unpleasantly again, as they had last night. Tricking her parents was one thing, but sneaking off with another scooter when she should be at drudge was another. She had come prepared: supposedly the scooter would break down, and she had lifted a burnt part from the recycle bin to display once she returned to the yard.

This scooter had a full charge, so she cranked speed up to max and sped along on the silent energy cushion until she reached the mountain. This time she parked away from the house, and walked up the drive.

The door slid open, and Miguel stood on the

threshold. "Philippa," he said quietly, smiling a welcome. The lenses were gone from his eyes, revealing the warm green she'd loved on Alphorion.

"Come in. It's safe," he murmured, standing aside.

"I can't stay long," she said. "I'm supposedly testing that scooter. But I wanted to find out if you are all right—and what happened?"

"This place was a wonderful idea," he said, smiling. "It's even got clothing of all sizes, and a cleaner and presser." He indicated the one-piece outfit he was wearing that seemed as if it had been made for his tall, broad-shouldered body. "What are these called? I noticed people wearing them in Gandria, and they are simple and comfortable. A pleasant change from Alphorion's elaborate formality, and the drab crewman's jumpers I've worn since!"

"They're called boormans," Philippa grinned, suppressing an urge to run her hands over the contours of his arms. "My parents hate them."

Miguel laughed, then said, "My only need now—and it's a crucial one—is for an omnilink coder." He gestured at the communications console built discreetly into a beautifully carved wood desk. "Right now it's set up for monolink only, calls in and calls out."

"Why is that a problem?" she asked. "You just don't answer any calls that might come in! You shouldn't be making any, either, if you're worried about traces."

"If I'd just wanted to get lost, I'd be out in your wilderness somewhere," he said with a soft laugh. "I need to be able to monitor planetwide communications for news, so I can figure out when—and how—I'm to get off this world again."

"What happened?" she asked again.

Miguel sank onto one of the low, plush couches. Philippa sat nearby.

"Better if you don't know the details," he said wryly. "But I—"

Philippa flushed. "I did *not* betray you when I was arrested!"

Miguel gave her a warm smile. "I know that. It's to protect *you*. We were desperately afraid after you disappeared. But nothing happened and no one came after us. The thing is, we *were* betrayed just before I left Alphorion. Do you remember Carl Albertin?"

"A few years older than me, curly black hair, always joking?" Philippa looked amazed. "I remember him. He was so friendly!"

"He sold our names to the government. Our cell and one other. He's probably landed, via state-paid ticket, on Felicidad by now." Miguel's voice remained soft, but he flexed his hands once, then put them in his lap. "Anyway, I was able to obtain false identification papers as a crew member aboard a transport. After Carl sold us out, when the League Peacekeepers came looking for me, I assumed this identity and hired on to the first ship that was available. By chance, it was coming here. When we arrived, the communications chief, who had become a friend of mine, said that the Planetary League had inquired about the crew list. Apparently they wanted to discuss—something— with the captain. I did not wait to find out what, but took the first transport sled out of Ambora, and lost myself in Gandria. I didn't know that there are only two cities on this planet!"

"How did you find me?"

"Purely by accident." He smiled at her. "I saw your parents walking through the Administrative Dome. I recognized your mother right away! I did some checking on the public codes over the next few days, and sent you the message via the school. I did not want to risk trying your home."

"Good thinking," she said, unable to hide the trace of bitterness in her voice.

Miguel's expression changed. "Was it bad?"

"Not bad if you don't mind ruining three people's lives." Her laugh came out shaky. "Never mind. I said I'd help you, and I will."

Now was the time for him to hold out his arms, to tell her how much she meant to him—but instead, he stood up. "I appreciate it, Philippa. We will someday gain our goal, and it will be because of loyal people like you. But I need that coder as soon as you can safely locate one."

Was he waiting for her to leave? Philippa stood slowly, hiding her disappointment. "It won't be easy. As you say, this is a small settlement, and everything's still owned and run by the Planning Committee—which is to say, the government. So any communications hardware and software, including replacement parts, are still handed out by the Planning Council."

"I see," he said quietly. "So you can't get a coder?"

Her disappointment changed to challenge. "I'll do it," she promised. "It just might take a bit of time."

He stepped next to her and lifted a hand, lightly

touching her hair. "That's the Philippa I remembered! It's so good to see someone from home," he murmured. "And it's good to see *you*."

Her eyes stung. *Nobody's ever said that to me before.* "I'll be back. As soon as I can get your coder." She left quickly.

Zach Yamoto's hand jerked, and he almost dropped his tray.

"Toroid!"

"Vacuum-head!"

Zach set his food down on the table carefully. He felt disoriented, and could barely take in the good-natured teasing of his younger brothers.

"Zach," called his mother. Zach glanced up quickly and saw the question in her eyes.

He gave her a lopsided grin. "I'm all right."

Dr. Yamoto lifted her fork, then put it down again as Lilith and Portia burst into a sudden argument about the villainous sidekick, Jezebel, in *Galaxy Patrol.* Both girls called on their mother to tell the other that she was right.

The chaos intensified as there was a beep on the comm-link, and Tris lunged toward the console before anyone could move. "It's mine!"

Commander Yamoto looked up from his dinner with mild interest. "A call from a young lady, Tris?"

"Yuck! Corrosive!" A moment later, he called in a deflated voice, "For you, Zach."

Zach got up. His brother lingered in the hallway, and hissed as he went by, "Hurry it up! I've got a high-pri call coming."

"Something good, I hope." Zach gave him an absent smile.

"Listen! Hissing! Villain-hissing Pippa missing

missing missing!" A theskie appeared suddenly in the doorway, adding its chatter to the hubbub caused by two separate and vigorous arguments.

"Heyo, Admiral!" Zach paused to rub the top of the creature's head. He sent a fast glance at the rest of the family, but they had paid the theskie no attention whatsoever. Zach heard his father laughing. In a moment, he'd probably get the squabbling kids to quiet down, but now Zach could focus on his call without being overheard.

He knew before he saw Clea's anxious brown eyes that she was the caller. There was a moment of silence while they studied each other's faces, then she asked, "Did you hear that? On the mental current?"

"I didn't hear anything," Zach murmured. "Felt it, though. Very strong, then cut off fast. It was Philippa, and I placed her somewhere to the west. That's all."

"Felt what?" Clea asked.

Zach hesitated, thinking back. "Hard to put into words. A couple of different things, but sadness sums it up best."

Clea's large brown eyes were serious. Watching them on the screen, Zach was vaguely aware of the range of colors in her eyes. Not just brown, but brown and green and gold and amber and . . . "I heard something," Clea said finally. "And it wasn't my thought. I heard, 'Nobody's ever said that to me before.' And the sadness. Then that was cut off. What's going on?"

Zach shook his head. "Can you locate Philippa right now?"

Clea's eyes took on an intent, inward stare for

long seconds, then she slowly shook her head. "You?"

"No, and trying makes my head feel like it did in the ion storm."

Clea sighed. "Let's talk to her tomorrow, when we meet to work on the model of the city. Maybe if she sees us, it will be easier to talk." Her voice ended on a hopeful note.

"Maybe!" Zach gave Clea a smile, but as they cut the line, he thought, *Not our Philippa.*

Zach stood up, and saw Tris fidgetting impatiently behind him. Tris pushed past him and punched a fast comm-code. As Zach walked away slowly, he heard Tris's urgent whisper behind him: "No one, huh? Well, that's a stone. Guess we'll have to go to the Toroid Plan . . .

Toroid Plan? Zach thought as he slid back into his seat at the table. *No. Won't ask. I don't think I want to know.*

Paul Riedel let himself out of the lab the next morning. He'd spent two hours trying to convince the scientists that he knew how to keep the silanna from disintegrating only to be told that his latest theory wouldn't work. "It was a good idea," Mrs. Matthews had explained kindly. "But fortifying the silanna as you suggest will result in silanna that's *too* hard. It would have no give, and the movement of a quake would destroy it."

Dr. Rilvh appeared to have forgotten that Paul was there. During Paul's entire explanation, he'd been poring over a printout.

Paul had said stiffly, "Thanks for listening to my idea," and left.

Determined not to return to his lab, he wandered

aimlessly onto the skywalk outside of the Research Dome. Below, he could see lines of kids of various ages, streaming in for early-shift school. Paul leaned against the railing, staring down into the thundering waterfall of the Tati River. From time to time, a brisk breeze blew some spray from the fall into his face. He had never felt so alone.

"Uh—Paul?" a tentative voice said.

For a moment, Paul thought he was dreaming. The voice was quiet, a kid's voice, nearly drowned out by the thunder of the waterfall.

"Paul?" The voice was slightly more insistent.

Paul turned and gazed with blank surprise at a boy his own age. He recognized the wide-spaced light-brown eyes of Zach Yamoto's younger brother, Tris. Tris was also fourteen, but to Paul, he was just one of the second Cohort herd-minds making a lot of noise at Bradbury. Paul had never had much of anything to say to kids of his own age.

"Paul," Tris said, "your brother is looking for you—"

"Stepbrother," Paul corrected automatically. "The only gene-related brother I might have, which is at this point problematical, is in utero."

Tris blinked, then took a deep breath. "Look, uh, Paul. I understand that you know the various holo-model programs."

"That's correct. You can sign up for a tutorial at the—"

"It's not that." Tris sent a hasty glance around them. Beside a pair of techs who were deep in conversation, there was no one else on the skywalk. "So you might know—or be able to learn—the program for vid enhancement?"

"Vid-enhance—you mean, as in making holovids?" Paul asked, his amazement growing. "Special effects?" As Tris nodded, he asked, "Why?"

"Because we're making a vid, of course," Tris said urgently. "Which is a high-pri secret. But we can't use the comp at the Rec Center unless someone knows the program. So we wondered if you'd like to join us."

Paul opened his mouth to refuse, then changed his mind. "Who's us?"

Tris named some kids unknown to Paul, then added, "Oh yes! And the new director's daughter, Daphne DeVries."

"I'll do it," said Paul.

EIGHT:

Hardware Blues

When Philippa woke up that day, the first thing she was aware of was a feeling of pressure around her head. It felt as if someone had embedded a wire around her skull, then had drawn it tight.

She heard a quiet, *"Quu! Quu!"* and reached over the side of her bed and felt the soft, fluffy scales of a quufer. She stroked the creature, and the *quuing* increased. She found it very soothing. She did not open her eyes immediately, but she knew that the quufer's hair was changing to the deep orange that seemed to signify pleasure.

Philippa now had three quufers. She thought of them as hers, even though the odd, faceless creatures were more independent than cats, moving in and out of the domes at will. Philippa had never tried shutting them in; these three appeared more and more frequently, and always came straight to her room. She could not recall having seen one in her parents' side of the dome, after the one time, a few days after they moved in, when her mother made the loco chase the creature outside.

Though she knew her parents would not care, if they even noticed, she still enjoyed the fact that the quufers preferred her. "And best of all," she murmured as she got up, "they don't talk—and don't spy."

She padded into the *bain* and took a hot, stinging shower. Usually that helped, but when she came out, the tightness was still there. She had deliberately imagined a gray fog between her and Sean, Clea, Zach, Arkady, and Will; they must not discover where she was going, or why.

"Omnilink coder," she sighed.

At the thought of more illegal activity, all the sick uncertainty of those days after the arrest flooded back, with none of the excitement she'd once felt. *He said I was loyal,* she thought as she dressed carefully in a soft-colored, plain outfit that would not attract attention. *I wonder if other loyal Leffies ever feel like this, like they'd just as soon never bother again? Maybe it's because I'm here instead of on Alphorion.*

Or maybe it was because she lived with silent, but daily, reminders of the blame for her earlier illegal activity. *No use in thinking about that.* Her mind returned to Miguel.

I'm sixteen, she thought as she picked up her school materials and walked to the door. *No longer fourteen. I'll get his coder chip, and I will not give him any more fourteen-year-old hysterical confrontations. Maybe this time he'll look past the loyal Leffie, and notice* me.

Tris and Paul walked down from the high skywalk while Tris started explaining the story that his gang wanted to make into a vid.

They neared the Bradbury School entrance and saw Will just going in. Will saw them at the same time and hurried toward them, exertion still showing in his jerky movements whenever he tried to move fast.

"Paul! Paul," Will called, breathing hard. "You'd already gone to bed when I got in last night, and I couldn't ask you then. Any chance we can use your lab today, late shift? What we need is the comp. Model design. Classmates and I."

"If you like," Paul said stiffly. "I won't be using it."

"Phew! Thanks." Will nodded, leaning against a railing. A moment later he straightened up, smiling crookedly. Paul and Tris turned, and both immediately spotted Daphne's long, waving magenta hair. She was in the midst of a group of kids converging on the school. She saw them and gave them all a friendly smile.

"Hey! Daphne!" Tris gave a yelp of pleasure and galloped toward her. Daphne stopped, and kids streamed around them as she and Tris talked.

Paul waited, his eyes on Daphne. One of her hands was clasping the wide brim of a hat that threatened to become airborne in the breeze. Her long hair was ruffling and rippling like a river of fire. Paul sighed, unaware he was doing so. She looked so wonderful to him.

"Guess I'd better get inside," Paul scarcely heard his stepbrother mumble, and Will moved away slowly.

Tris ran back to Paul. Looking suspiciously after Will, he muttered, "Did you tell him anything? He's in with Zach and them, and he was standing there so long—"

"Of course not!" Paul had not even noticed Will's presence.

"Good." Tris looked relieved. "Now. Daphne says we can meet her at the Rec Center at midshift, if you're free. She'll tell us what equipment we'll need, and for how long."

Paul smiled. "I believe I can postpone my project at the tidal generator site until late shift—"

"Then meet us there!" Tris interrupted again. "Gotta flash!"

Philippa used her code word to shut the loco down. As she bent over the communications console, she spoke out loud. "Philippa, dear." She imitated her mother's voice as her fingers lifted the casing and then began moving quickly among the wires and tiny solid-state chips. "You'd do well to remember that anyone who betrays an interest in manual labor will be tracked into menial jobs for life."

Philippa paused, picking up one of the fine silver instruments that she kept in a slim folder in her school materials. Lowering her voice in a comic imitation of her father's precise, clipped accents, she went on: "You still don't seem to realize that the track we have selected for you at the academy, Philippa, will train you to assess data and make appropriate decisions. You will do best to learn at once that the maintenance of data-collecting machinery is a delta-level job. If you display too much interest in such pursuits, other alpha-level peers will shun you for having delta-level interests. And you will never advance if your peers regard you with contempt. Ah!" She stopped, pulling up a chip and carefully bending it. "Still perfectly good, but if *they* come home early, *they* will take one look and assume it's hopeless."

She turned to the loco. "Loco," she said calmly, watching it reactivate, "I am going to school. The comm-link is down. The repair-person has been called."

"Have a pleasant day, dear Phi—"

She was out the door before the loco could finish its phony message.

She stopped near Bradbury and used a public comm-link to call her father's office. Her face was bland as the screen blinked and showed her father's assistant. He looked mildly curious. "Good morning, Philippa. Do you need to talk to your father?"

"Oh, please don't disturb him!" she said sweetly. "Just let him know that our home comm-link is malfunctioning. I called a repair person, who promised us a high-pri rating. We should be on line by late shift, I was told. I just want you to inform him in case he tries to call home." She gave the young man a brilliant smile. He grinned in response. "I'm also late for school. *Would* you let my mother know about the problem?"

"Sure, Philippa!"

"Thanks so much, Thann."

They cut the line, and she smiled. Her parents would never think to check into that. They had made it very clear that machinery was a topic for bores, and once they'd expressed their dislike for those classes in hardware design she'd elected to take, she knew they had assumed she dropped them at once. Well, she hadn't dropped them. She'd just never mentioned them again.

As she walked down the pathway next to the Tati

River, her mind veered: She suddenly remembered a date she'd had with Sean. They'd stood together over the waterfall between the huge, moonlit domes of the city center, talking idly about how a hoverscooter might be altered to ride the river. Sean had been delighted to discover someone else who enjoyed poking about machines, finding unexpected (or unregulated) capabilities—but then his interest had pushed beyond that to her past. . . .

She winced, hurrying her steps. Unable to deal with his persistent questions about her former planet, she'd picked an argument with him over where to go for a snack, then cut the date short. He'd been mad at her for a few days afterward, but that was better than his finding out the truth. She remembered those long weeks after the arrest, when not one of her friends had so much as sent a message.

Why should anyone here be any different? *Sean Matthews, governor's duty-minded son. Dating a criminal from Alphorion? Impossible.* She had also been careful to never mention any interest in mechanics again.

Her insides lurched as she recalled the night of the storm, and what she'd told Arkady. *Why did I do that?* she thought furiously. She had avoided Arkady as much as possible since, afraid of further questions—or that he'd somehow use her past against her.

Suddenly she wasn't seeing the path in front of her feet. There in her mind, clear as if she stared through his eyes, was an image of the tutor robot in school. And even closer, Arkady's well-shaped, strong hands and his portable terminal—

Philippa stopped short, feeling vertigo. *Don't.*

Don't. She admonished herself fiercely, trying to surround her thoughts with gray fog again. The current was definitely getting stronger, catching her whenever she was off-guard. *Don't relax again, vacuum-skull!*

The Administrative Dome was ahead. Philippa walked swiftly inside and down the hallways until she reached the huge Communications Systems Supply Department. *Let's just get this over with fast.*

She summoned up a bland, slightly bored smile and mentally rehearsed her prepared tale—but it all ran out of her head as the door slid open and she was face to face with her mother's technical aide.

"Philippa!"

"Hi, Hannah." Philippa forced a smile to her lips.

"What brings you over here?" the secretary asked in surprise.

Philippa tossed her hair back. "Oh, the comm-link dumped on me this morning. I called for repair, and the tech is one of our school aides. I said I'd get a part for her. So we'll be on line before my parents get home and need it—"

"Philippa."

Philippa whirled around, staring at her mother. She started her story again, until she saw by the slight lift to her mother's pale, perfect brows that she had little interest in the comm-link repair. She cut herself off abruptly.

"Why are you not in school?" her mother asked, looking bored.

"I will be. I have to get something for a lab anyway," Philippa said desperately. She did not want to lie outright and say she had classes, when this was her free-study morning. It would be too easy for her mother to check that—and then wish to check further.

Her mother lifted a hand. "It was very thoughtful of you to arrange the console repair so expediently. As it happens, I was going to send you a message as soon as I returned to the office: You'll remember that your father and I were scheduled to dine out this evening. I did not discover until this morning that families are expected."

Philippa stared, only habit keeping her face bland.

"We'll have to leave as soon after the late shift as can be arranged," her mother murmured. As Philippa did not speak, her brows rose again. "Philippa?"

"I was wondering what to wear," Philippa said quickly.

"Early evening. Terrace." Director Bidding turned. "Hannah? Are we ready? Have a pleasant day, my dear. We shall see you at home."

"Have a pleasant day," Philippa called, moving away slowly.

Getting the omnilink coder was easy, as it turned out. The disinterested assistant was some older teen doing drudge. Philippa did not know him. As soon as she gave her family's personal code, the green light blinked on the console and she soon had the little chip.

So that was easy. What remained now was to get the comm-link at home reinstalled, and to get the part to Miguel.

She had planned to spend the rest of the morning fixing the comm-link, and tonight, when her parents were at their Planning Committee dinner, she'd rush out to the retreat house to get rid of the chip.

Now what?

Her steps took her toward Bradbury as her mind worked furiously.

"Well, *that's* over!" Clea slammed the case shut on her school materials. "Whew, that was dull! Structure of sugars. Just what I need for everyday living!"

"Everyday living suggests sustenance," a kid nearby said.

"Something sweet," Zach Yamoto spoke at Daphne's side. Daphne turned around as she clapped her hat on her head. "Ah, fair maid! My heart misgives!" Zach proclaimed, bowing.

"Get thee hence, varlet." Daffy whipped off her hat again and waved it languidly in his face.

"Oh, fair torment! That the sweetness I crave is forever denied. Cruel, cruel!" Zach clasped his hands to his heart, dropping on his knees before Daphne.

"Remove thy foul presence, 'ere I summon the lackeys!" Daphne, never one to refuse a challenge, replied grandly.

A boy she didn't know cupped his fingers around his mouth and squeaked in a theskie-like voice, "Lackeys? Lackeys?"

Daphne settled her hat on her head, grinning. She noticed Will watching, his strong-boned face wide and attractive as he smiled. She found it intriguing that Will's laugh was entirely inward.

"This corridor is an accessway, not a gathering place." A sarcastic voice doused the fun from behind.

The kids turned guiltily to see Mr. Santori, the school's assistant director, standing there. "Have you nothing to do?" he asked with seeming surprise. "If so, there are plenty of assignments that need filling." Most of the crowd began melting away, as Mr. Santori frowned. "Was that you again, Yamoto, causing a disturbance?"

"Not a disturbance, sir," Zach said. "We were just joking around."

"Then joke elsewhere," Santori snapped. After a glance at Daphne that made her wonder if she'd bathed that morning, he walked away.

"Corrosion!" Zach said under his breath.

"Squared and cubed!" Will responded. He'd ducked into a doorway. "Come on, let's catch up with the others." Daphne saw his eyes resting on her, though he seemed to be talking to Zach.

"Sustenance! Before the shackles of midshift drudge," Zach said. "Coming, Daffy, my delight?"

Daphne laughed. "I wish! I made plans for midshift."

They were walking toward the front door. Will began talking easily about the science assignment, then suddenly fell silent.

Glancing to the side, Daphne saw Zach's brow furrowed, his usually smiling mouth solemn. Both boys were staring through the crowd toward a slim, pale-haired girl—Philippa Bidding. She was talking earnestly to a girl whose name Daphne did not know. Daphne could not mistake the interest the boys showed; Philippa looked up and saw them coming. Her face seemed oddly blank.

"Hi, Pippa," Zach called.

For a second, it seemed as if Philippa would turn without speaking to them. She stopped, though, and said, "Hi, everyone. Zach, Will, could you—let the others know? I'm not feeling well, and I think I'd better go home. My parents expect me to go with them to a party this evening." Philippa was talking rapidly. Her face looked even more pale than usual, and there were faint strain shadows around her eyes.

"Sure. We'll tell them," Zach said mildly.

Philippa hurried off. Daphne walked a bit farther, then she also took her leave of the silent boys with a careless wave of her hand.

Is that girl weird, or are they all weird about her? she wondered as she walked along the path to the Rec Center. *All of them?* She thought of Will's silent laughter.

Ahead, she saw Tris standing with a small group of kids. This time Will's stepbrother, the one who seemed to like ballet, was with them. He was gazing at her silently.

"Come over to the Rec Center," she heard herself say briskly. "If you can tell me a little about your project, then maybe I can help."

NINE:

Theskies, Theskies Everywhere

Paul watched Daphne. She was gazing at the console in front of her, with fingers tapping its edge slightly. Paul knew she did not hear Tris and his friends' loud argument going on around her. *She thinks we're babies.*

Well, he'd show her that *he* was different.

"Look," he cut into the angry voices. "I agreed to help you, but I can do little if you don't adhere to even rudimentary logic."

Jehanne, a short, round girl with lots of curly dark hair and intense dark eyes, frowned at him. "What's that supposed to mean?"

"But he's right," Tank interrupted. Tank was the muscular one with spiky hair. "I *told* you that. Pirate ships didn't make fuel stops: they ran on wind power! Those sails weren't just for decoration!"

"Hah!" Mik jabbed a skinny finger toward Tank,

who was at least twice his weight. "There you're wrong, numb-nose. We've got a vid showing those old ships with paddlewheels, and smoke belching up from the engine room!"

"The earlier ones predated engines," Paul informed them.

"You oughta ask your brother. He's always rummaging through ancient vids and flatpics and things—" Tank poked Tris.

"No." Tris glared at his friend. "We're not asking any of *them*!"

Daphne jumped. "Hey. A little less noise, all right? What's wrong?"

Paul said, "I merely attempted to point out fundamental flaws in the progression of the action, as envisioned by—"

"It's a good story," Jehanne interrupted. "So we messed up a little on the history."

"Here." Daphne smiled, silencing them all. "I can't get what you need until you can tell me what's going to happen in your vid. I suggest you come back when you've worked out your disagreements."

The others left, but Paul lingered. Once again, Daphne was staring at the console. Paul cleared his throat. As she jumped, startled, he said hastily, "May I, uh, help with anything?"

Daphne smiled at him. "No thanks, Paul. See you later!"

Paul. She said his name. Paul felt his heart doing things that were supposed to be physically impossible according to the anatomy books.

"Bye," he said, and he somehow managed to get himself out, despite the six extra arms and legs he seemed to have grown.

Clea and the others walked to the Greendome eatery with a group from their class, but somehow the five friends ended up alone at a small table. The expressions on Zach's and Will's faces when they caught up with the other three had drawn the gang together almost automatically.

"Our renegade wench hath begged off from our gathering today," Zach said as soon as they all had their food.

"Why?" Sean asked sharply.

"Said she's sick," Will answered. "Has to rest before a party this evening."

"Well, that last part is true," Sean muttered. "Planning Committee bash. Couple of rankers from Gandria are visiting. I was told yesterday that this is a family 'Will Attend, Will Have Fun' official event. That means I'll be there as well." He smiled grimly. "Maybe I can find some time for a little talk with Miss Bidding."

Clea felt cold all of a sudden. "She's in some kind of trouble," she burst out. "Can't you feel it?"

Zach gave a wry grin. "I did. Maybe jug time with my mother wasn't so corrosive after all. I've only had two sessions with her, but first thing she wanted me to learn was how to block out the mental stuff you don't want to hear. I think just today I'm getting it, and for the first time since the day Pippa stole the craft, I haven't been getting bombardments of bad current from her."

"Bad current," Will repeated slowly. "It *is* kind of like an electrical current between us all, isn't it? With no on or off toggles?"

Zach nodded. "And it's bad when I keep getting someone else's tension and can't do anything about it."

"Philippa's," Sean said. "So something is definitely wrong with her."

"This is really scary," Clea said quietly.

"Not as scary as the thought of who else might be getting current from us," Arkady put in suddenly.

"As in a villain who hunts illegally?" Sean looked grim.

"Or non-humans." Clea's topaz eyes were intense. "*Some*thing caused us to start getting it, and I don't think it could have been any of the other colonists!"

"This brings us right back to trying to solve it," Sean said. "*And* Philippa's non-cooperation. If she is in trouble, why doesn't she tell us?" Sean glared around the table. "Maybe I'm too cranked to feel anything but a strong desire to dunk her in the canal! Look, first she misappropriates an official vehicle. All right, maybe there was a reason. We all know what that's like." He shrugged. Clea thought back to the terrible storm, and Sean, Arkady, and Philippa out searching for one another, pulled by this mental bond. "But when we cover for her, she shoos us out like we were household rodents. What's going on?" His eyes narrowed angrily. "My dad once told me to see a little less of her. Not that I'd listen to that sort of thing ordinarily, but—"

"Something did happen once," Arkady said slowly. "Whatever it was seems to have left her unable to trust anyone."

"She's not feeling mean; she's feeling scared!" Clea put in.

"Scared and sad and hopeful and tense," Zach added, nodding. "So what do we do?"

"I think it would be horrid to pounce on her like some kind of patrol squad and demand answers,"

Clea said. "Why don't we try to talk to her as individuals?"

"Maybe a party is not a good place," Sean said. "But I've got construction drudge with her now. Maybe she'll show for that."

"And I'll try tomorrow after physics," Clea said.

"Sounds good—" Zach was interrupted by the bell that the shop proprietor had installed for the Bradbury students.

"Meet you at Paul's lab at late shift!" Will waved.

Clea watched the others rush out. She had midshift free today, so she finished her cocoa more slowly, then got up to leave. Her thoughts crashed around in her brain without getting anywhere. Sean, Philippa, the weird city on the plateau, this mental bond that no one else in Ambora seemed to have.

He was really mad at Philippa. Clea did not make the mistake of thinking that that meant he had lost interest in her. Just the opposite. She'd seen him quarrel with Philippa and then date her the next week, over and over.

On Galahad, I never had any problems finding dates, Clea thought ruefully. But Galahad had been so different—and Sean was so different from all the boys she had known back home. She had been attracted to him from the instant she woke up from the deep-space sleep and saw his green eyes and long dark eyelashes. At first it had seemed he was equally attracted to her. *Maybe he is a little, but it's a mild, unexciting sort of thing,* she thought sadly as she walked toward home. *Philippa's exciting, even when she makes him mad.*

She reached home to find that both her parents had the midshift free as well. They greeted her, and her father asked if he could punch up some more of the exotic stew substitute that the new menu card offered.

Clea summoned up a smile. "No, thanks. I just had a snack."

"Sit down then." Her father gestured to her place. "Your sisters are at school, which provides us with a rare opportunity for conversation that does not hinge on the recent machinations of Rotten Rupert and the ever-sinister Jezebel."

Clea tried to grin.

"Do you feel all right?" her mother asked with concern.

"Oh, Mom." A feeling of fondness for her parents rushed through Clea, easing a little of the hurt. "I guess I'm worried about a friend."

"Log and enter: Concerned Dad Routine, program 223-A. Starts: Anything I can do . . ." Dr. Tourni intoned, gazing skyward.

Clea grinned, and leaned over to kiss him on the cheek. "I copy! But I think I can handle it. If I can't, I'll log and enter: Howling Daughter program 1000!"

"We'll howl together," her mom promised. "And howl is what I'd like to do over this stuff. Stew! I remember real stew on Galahad." She shook her head morosely, then looked up when the panel on the wall buzzed softly. "Ah! Comm-link. Who of us has been saved from finishing his or her plate? Would you find out, Clea?"

"Sure." Clea got up and moved into the little room that held the family's comm-link console. To her surprise, the face that came on the screen belonged to Sean Matthews. Behind him, Clea could see an edge of park and new construction. He was calling from a public unit. "Sean?"

"Philippa isn't here," he said grimly. "She got one of the girls from the classical-lit class to cover for her—said she had an emergency at home. Didn't she tell Zach and Will she was sick?"

Clea sighed, nodding.

"Can you find her with the current?"

Clea shook her head slowly.

Sean frowned. "I'm tempted to call the Med Center and her home, just to find out which—if either—is the truth."

Clea shook her head. "Go ahead, if you think you need to."

After they'd cut the line, Clea went into her room and curled up on her bed, staring up at the ceiling. *Face it, Clea Tourni,* she thought. *Sean Matthews definitely has Philippa Bidding on the mind. Meanwhile, you've got to meet with them all in half a shift! Forget Sean. Think about that city. . . .*

A soft form nudged her hand suddenly, and she turned over to see a quufer next to her bed. She smiled and pulled the creature up, cuddling its fluffy body next to her. She watched, feeling oddly comforted, as the quufer's furry scales slowly changed to a deep orange.

She was not aware of falling asleep: She was just vaguely aware of being back on the high plateau, with the other five, the sound of that voice in her mind, its call unrelenting: *Come and bear witness!*

The scene changed: She saw the city again, and the inhabitants. . . . She saw the sudden fear and chaos . . . and through it, Philippa calling: *I'm alone, I'm alone.*

"Uh!" She sat up, feeling cold and frightened.

The quufer was still beside her, but it was no longer *quuing* happily. Its furry scales were a strange, dull green.

Clea glanced at the chrono. Late shift soon! She took a hasty shower and dressed in a fresh boorman. This time she did not try to guess what Sean might think flattering; she just picked the first one at hand.

As she let herself out the door, she saw a theskie leaping on the grass. "Missy-missy-missing! Missing!" It chattered on a high note, its orange eyes glittering in the strong afternoon sunlight.

"Missing! You've been saying that for a couple of days. Do you like that sound? Try kissing!" She touched its head.

"Kissing missing!"

"You got that right." Clea laughed ruefully. "No, don't get underfoot; I've got to go."

She set out at a fast walk, but as if her hurry had attracted them, she found she soon had three theskies running beside or across the skywalks, their tails twitching back and forth rapidly.

By the time she reached the student lab area of the Research Dome, she discovered that she had a train of seven of the reptilian creatures.

Zach and Arkady were waiting outside the door. Zach laughed when he saw her entourage. "What, been feeding them?" he joked.

"No. I think my being in a hurry makes them think I'm trying to play," she groaned. "Shoo! We have work to do!"

Instead of shooing, the theskies ran up and down the hall, poking their heads into every door or alcove they saw and touching any object in reach with their clawed fingers. All seven were yapping shrilly, their words impossible to understand.

Will and Sean arrived together, and as soon as Will opened the door to his brother's lab the theskies shoved their way in first.

"Who invited them?" Sean demanded in exasperation. "How are we going to hear each other talk?"

Zach said easily, "Oh, they liked Clea rushing over. Maybe if we're quiet, they'll get bored and leave. Will, you doing the honors?"

"Guess I can," Will said, settling awkwardly onto Paul's high-seated chair. "I'll sketch in the contours of the plateau first. Then let's each take turns suggesting one specific thing we noticed."

The kids were silent, trying to think; the theskies continued to run about, touching and picking things up. They did not make a mess, but Clea noticed Will looking up anxiously from time to time.

Sean had pinched his fingers over his eyes, and was frowning deeply. Zach was slouched in a chair, feet out and hands dangling over the sides. His eyes were lightly closed. Arkady stared at a wall, his body still and tense.

Clea's mind went back to the weird dream she'd just had. *Forget that,* she thought. *Get your mind back to the day we were lost. . . .*

She tried to retrace their actions. Waking up the last night in the mountains. Arguing with Sean about the safety of leaving the camp. Leaving camp. Being drawn to the plateau. And doing the impossible—entering the solid wall of the mountain . . .

Sean getting angry. Sean being worried. Sean when he first got his mental message: *Come and bear witness!*

Philippa frightened but somehow trusting the message . . .

Clea sat up, shaking her head. *Come on, girl!* she chided herself. *Think about the city!*

But her mind ran right back to images of her friends' faces during those emotional moments before they made the discovery.

Finally she looked up in despair—to find Zach slowly shaking his head. "No go, either?" he addressed Clea. "I keep seeing the city's destruction."

"I keep seeing us running, before that last quake struck and destroyed the plateau," Arkady murmured.

Sean shrugged. "And I was seeing Clea and Zach when they were fighting off that monster lizard."

Will rubbed his eyes. "Everything that led up to it, or happened afterward. Maybe to visualize the city itself, we need all six of us."

"Maybe it was just a mass halucination after all," Zach said softly.

"You don't believe that any more than I do," Sean said. "Remember how long it took to convince me while it was happening? I don't have any questions about its reality. I don't see why we can't—"

"We're trying too hard," Arkady interjected, "and their noise isn't helping." He pointed to the theskies still scrambling about the lab, apparently fascinated with making the door hiss open and closed. "We're trying to see the city, *and* to find Philippa. I don't think we can do two things at once."

"Then we drop the city until we've had a talk with Philippa," Sean said grimly.

"First let's take a break and think of *fun* things,"

Zach suggested, standing up and stretching. "Did you copy the notice in the IRC today? About the dance Director DeVries is organizing for the incoming settlers?"

Will grinned. "Maybe I'll ask Daphne for details!"

Clea followed the boys out slowly. When she looked up, it was to see Sean standing next to her. She looked up at him, and suddenly she knew what was coming.

"Want to make the dance a date?" Sean asked, smiling into her eyes.

Clea fought a sudden lump in her throat and won. A little spurt of anger helped. "Why? We'll just spend the evening talking about Philippa, and we do that all day anyway. I think I'd rather try my luck with one of the newbies."

Her voice went high at the end, but she got out the door and down the hall, theskies clattering behind her, without anyone seeing her face.

TEN:

Love and Duty

Philippa rubbed her temples slowly as the spacious Bidding hovercraft raced over the road. At least this time she had taken her own family's vehicle. She knew it was unlikely her mother or father would need it before the end of late shift; if she rushed out and back, she might also have just enough time to recharge the power before she returned it to the Administrative Dome lot.

And if I get caught, will they turn me in as a thief? Thinking about that was somehow less upsetting than thinking about the gang. *At least it would all be over.* She sat up straight, mentally scolding herself. *Toroid! It's not over, and you chose to answer Miguel's message, and who says the others will even notice if you're scarce for a few days?*

She tried to steady herself with logic, but what disturbed her most was that moment when she had without warning seen *through* Arkady's eyes. That defied logic. It defied emotion as well, for some reason she did not want to pursue. "I'll think about Miguel," she said firmly.

Miguel was waiting for her when she drove up to the safe house. As she stepped out of the car, she held up her fist with the chip in it, and Miguel's smile made it all suddenly worth it. "'O rare and wonderful!'" he greeted her. "'Avian thout compare.'"

Philippa laughed, following him inside. "Avian? Isn't that a monkey?"

"That's simian. Avians are birds—and here, a bird of paradise." He smiled back over his shoulder as he moved to the communications console.

Philippa, delighted, stopped very close to him. "I just left a scene like this at home." She touched the console.

"Did you have to hobble your home system?" Miguel asked as he carefully lifted delicate wires.

"Just disabled it for a while, in order to get the extra part with no questions asked. Here, I also brought these." She held out her packet of tiny instruments.

Miguel caught her hand and kissed it, an old Alphorion custom. Now a thrill ran straight through her. "Thank you! There is little even remotely useful in this place. It must indeed be a retreat. I nearly had to make do with eating utensils when I dismantled the system."

Philippa found she couldn't meet his eyes. "Shall I help?"

"Please."

Working together, they soon had the console operational. Miguel did not turn it on immediately, though. As he slid the last of her instruments into the folder, he asked, "How long can you stay?"

"A short time." Philippa explained about the hovercraft.

Miguel nodded. "Good idea," he said. "I was right to trust you." And as Philippa smiled happily at him, he went on in the formal tones of Alphorion, "May I offer you any refreshment? They seem to have an excellent stock here, though I have been careful."

"Just something cold to drink."

Miguel dialed an exotic fruit juice for them both, then sat down on one of the comfortable chairs. Philippa would have rather sat with him on the couch, but she sank into the other chair. "Is it boring up here?" she asked, sipping the tangy drink.

Miguel turned to stare out the long western window. The Kartai Sea sparkled, a phosphorescent gray-blue, straight out to the far horizon. "Boring?" he repeated. "Not that. Quiet, certainly. But I've welcomed the opportunity to sit and think in relative safety. To examine questions and answers that I had no time for until now." He turned and smiled at her. "Have you found it the same, living here? Have you thought about coming back when you are of age?"

"Coming back to Alphorion?" she asked, her heart thumping hard. "As?"

He glanced over in mild surprise. "As yourself. Your value to us would be increased, not diminished, if you're thinking that the arrest would change that. You proved your loyalty to the cause."

Loyalty to you. Can't you see it? She stared somberly into the dark blue depths of her drink. *I guess I have to say it.*

"I'd like to have value to you," she said softly.

"You do." Miguel set aside his drink and moved

to kneel by her chair. His spring-green eyes were steady and earnest as he touched her shoulder lightly. "Are you angry with me for not trying to find out what had happened to you? For not sending a message?" He hesitated for a moment, as if choosing his words carefully. "For a long time, I knew nothing at all. There were no witnesses to your arrest, or if there were, the League Peacekeepers prevailed on them not to talk to the newscasters. By the time we found out, word leaked through that your parents had elected to resign their positions and emigrate. We were sure that your home system was monitored at all times, and there was always the chance that you had talked, or were so angry with us that you'd turn us in if we contacted you. And," he said quietly, "I hope you'll forgive me, but no one quite wanted to ask your parents to take a personal message to you."

"It would have been a waste of time." Philippa looked at him searchingly. During the long ride out to the house, she had enjoyed a wonderful daydream. It featured Miguel taking her into his arms, and proposing marriage. He would take her back to Gandria, and they would find a way to get off the planet and back to Alphorion. She could send one last, triumphant message to her parents: *Good-bye.* Then, on Alphorion, she and Miguel would work side by side for the freedom of their home planet.

She realized slowly that what she was trying to do now was separate Miguel from the Leffie cause, and get him to respond to her personally. Was it even possible? What was he like, when not doing Leffie work? Did he like holovids, or music, or off-world cuisine, or dancing? Those were the things she wanted to begin finding out.

But as she looked at Miguel, she realized he had nothing but the cause on his mind. She'd dated enough boys to recognize all the little signals when one wanted more than casual friendship. Holding hands almost always came first: An aggressive boy would take hers, if she placed them encouragingly near his; a shy boy would have his hands where she could reach them if she wanted to make the first move.

Miguel's hands were there, but one was a light fist on one knee, and the other rested on the back of her chair. His face was near hers, but that expression could just as easily be one he'd give a male friend who was having doubts about himself, or about the movement.

He's trying to bolster my self-opinion, she thought Immediately, the ironic part of her mind added promptly, *which is exactly the wrong way to do it.*

Looking at his kindly, concerned expression was suddenly unbearable. She got up and wandered to the window. "The sea looks peaceful from here, but did you know that there's a two-hundred-foot tidal range?"

Miguel was not fooled. "What is it? Something's wrong," he said. "You are still angry with us?"

"I promise you that I'm not." Philippa took a deep breath. "I've a new start here, is all. I just don't know what I'm going to do when I come of age." She turned her back to the window. "Did you . . . leave anyone behind?"

"Leave anyone?" Miguel got up slowly, then sank back into his chair.

"Anyone special," she added before he could

enumerate his companions in the organization.

"Oh." He shot her a quizzical look. "Technically, I suppose I did. My parents designated me at birth for marriage into the Trowbridge family—you know how it is."

Philippa nodded. "None better. My parents are both descended from the Bidding cousins who first set up the Planetary Secretariat, and they were engaged at age fifteen. There was some talk of my cousin Geoffrey Bidding for me; my first horrible fight with my parents was when I refused. I was ten then. He snuffled a lot, and I once saw him doing mean things to a stray cat."

Miguel smiled. "I met him once at the Youth Academy. I don't blame you. Well, Annabelle Trowbridge isn't quite so repulsive, and besides, I needed a vacuum-sealed excuse to be in and out of the Salle de Justice so frequently. But our dates were entirely taken up with her non-stop descriptions of parties and clothes. One night," he laughed suddenly, "I tried not saying anything the entire evening, just to see if she'd notice. At the end, she told me the two things that made her think our marriage would work were that we shared the same ambitions, and I was a good listener!"

Philippa laughed with him, and she felt slightly better.

"I don't think she had much heart to lose," Miguel went on. "But as for me . . . I don't think I have a heart to give, either. Not to a person, when it already belongs to the planet." He smiled up at her, his eyes questioning. "Is that what you're asking?"

He looked so handsome, sitting there staring straight at her. *But he's told me fairly,* Philippa realized, *he's not for me.*

So now she knew. And, no matter what anyone said, the truth *hurt.* But she'd learned early how to hide her feelings: Old habit got her mouth to smile, and her voice to remain smooth. "I just wondered if grown-up Leffies ever have time for old musicals or eating chocolate gateaus," she said lightly. "Will you need anything more from me?"

Miguel's voice was quiet. "I hope to be gone soon. If there's no hue and cry on the communication bands, then I might try to see if I can crew out on the colonist ship that's now in orbit. Otherwise . . . if you think there's any danger—to you, if not to me—I can leave now."

"I have to go to a Planning Committee party tonight," Philippa said, setting down her glass. "Maybe someone'll mention a transport ship or something that needs a crew member. If so, I'll come tell you."

He nodded. "Thanks again." He did not hold out his hands.

"Bye, Miguel." She left quickly.

Both moons were out—one low and hanging just above the dark mountains, and the other high and small—when Sean and his parents left the party. *So much for talking to Philippa,* Sean thought in disgust as he climbed into his seat in the hovercraft. *They must teach those Alphorion society kids young how to completely avoid someone at a party.* He could still hear the faint sound of music, light chattering voices, and the tinkle of crystal glasses coming from the terrace on the hillside.

"A lovely house for entertaining, but I would not want to live with those stairs every day," Sean's mother said. "However, Sandra insisted we design the house on just that plan. I wonder if she's regretted it yet."

Sean's father chuckled. "I noticed she has two servo-bots. Must have done some brisk trading."

"Still on the luxury list?"

"Once we get our power sources stabilized, we'll be able to relax the pioneer rations," Mr. Matthews said. "Sean. Why the moody look? You're off the criminal list, you know, as of tomorrow, with driving privileges fully restored."

"Looking forward to it," Sean said tersely.

"You're not still angry with me? I hated to do it but I felt—"

"An example. Governor's son. Haven't forgotten that either, Dad." A sudden urge made him add: "Speaking of which. You once told me to stay away from Philippa Bidding. You never told me why."

There was a brief silence, then Sean's father said, "*Hmmmph.*" That could have meant anything. Sean wished he could see his father's face—then realized, he would not have asked that question if they'd been sitting around the table in the brightly lit kitchen at home. *I should be asking her,* he thought. *Anything else is sneaking.* "Ah, never mind," Sean said quickly.

"You haven't been seeing much of her lately, have you?" Governor Matthews commented wryly. "It occurs to me that this evening, for instance, you two were usually on opposite sides of the room."

"You probably woke up one morning after a nightmare in which Joan and Allen Bidding had suddenly become your in-laws." Mrs. Matthews laughed. They drew up in front of their dome, and the lights went on inside, glowing warmly through the windows. She added as they got out of the hovercraft, "And if *either* of you *ever* repeat that, *you'll* wake up scalped and stuffed."

"It's a glorious, glorious day!" Daphne DeVries sang the next morning as she drove into the parking lot at the Spaceport Complex. The sun was shining brightly and there was a soft, cool breeze blowing from the ocean, but that was not the cause of her joy. Today would be the first time she tried her new duty: As daughter of Director DeVries, she was on the Welcome Committee for greeting new colonists.

Entering the spaceport's waiting area, which had been cleared of the usual jumble of cargo slated for ground transport or lift-off, she saw Sean Matthews's tall form. He looked up and saw her at the same moment, grinning when he recognized her.

"You look like a picture," he said with a smile.

Daphne performed an expert curtsey. She was wearing a special outfit that she had brought from Felicidad, her home planet and holovid capital of the inner worlds: a dress with a wide skirt, a tight waist, and lacey neck and sleeves. The colors were gold and white, with a cherry sash that exactly matched the color of her hair. "Why not? A party dress makes a party spirit!"

"I'll try to remember that." Sean grinned wryly. "Maybe if I dressed up, this duty'd feel less like drudge."

Daphne had just been about to describe her enjoyment at her first time on the committee, but Sean's comment made the words freeze in her throat. *That's right*, she thought. *To you, it's just more outsiders coming*.

The silence was filled by a man's voice behind them. "Nice day for a landing, eh, kids?"

"Nice day for surfing, I was thinking," Sean replied. "Daphne, have you met Commander Yamoto? Daphne DeVries."

Daphne found herself looking up into his wide-spaced, keen gray eyes. Commander Yamoto was an older man, with a trim wiry body, thinning light hair, and the same wide smile that his children had. "Pleasure to meet you," she murmured.

"Pleasure to meet you, youngster," Commander Yamoto responded. "I must admit I've wanted to see this lovely young lady that Zach has described with such enthusiasm. I didn't know there was any-one alive who knew more quotations from obscure bits of historic entertainment than Zach." He winked at her. "And it's been good for him to find a wit quicker than his!"

Daphne laughed, suddenly liking this man. She'd heard that Commander Yamoto had retired with honors from the Planetary League Patrol, but had chosen to settle on this new world with his family. He was now in charge of all planetary communica-tions. She would have expected that someone with his formidable list of qualifications would be silent and dour, but he seemed friendly and accessible.

"Elected to the Welcome Committee, too?" She smiled up at him. "This is my first landing!"

"Not this time," Commander Yamoto said easily. "Merely here to greet an old crony who's in for a visit. I must say, the boys at least will find you a wel-coming sight. You might get drafted every time!"

"If there are boys, I'll be here!" Daphne grinned. Feeling suddenly confident, she turned to Sean. "I was thinking on my way over. If there are kids who'll be in our cohort at school, why not host a beach party for them? The weather's fine, tomorrow's a free day, and everyone would get a chance to meet new people. It's *awful* to feel left out."

"Sounds—"

Sean's response was drowned by a loud buzzer, followed by the muted thunder of the approaching shuttle. Daphne lost him in the rush to the greeting areas; afterward, she was too busy trying to remember the little speech she had to give to each person she was assigned, plus trying to answer all the questions of the curious, disoriented newcomers, to find Sean again.

The day passed with lightning speed, but Daphne finished by seeing her three families to their waiting domes. She showed them how to work the preparators, and where the storage areas were, and said at least a hundred times: "You'll find all that out at the orientation meeting tomorrow morning. Your meeting time is on this schedule, and a map of Ambora is here on the console!"

When she finally approached the small dome she shared with her father, she saw that it was dark inside. Her father, of course, worked at night mostly.

She let herself in. The lights came on, but the room was quiet. She remembered coming home on Felicidad, hearing—always—voices, music, laughter, smelling her mother's exotic scent . . .

"Delete sniffles, Daffo-my-duck," she said out loud. "I wonder if there are any kids my age in this landing?" There had been no time to ask, and her three families had all had a child or two, but none over the age of six.

As she passed toward the kitchen, she noticed

the blinking light on the console. Going over, she saw a message attached to her code.

"Hi, Daphne, this is Sean. No time to call back—my parents have me scheduled for more official fun this evening. Just wanted to thank you for the great idea, and to tell you that we've put out the word: tomorrow, beach, late shift. The new kids on the list will have been through their orientations by then. See you!"

ELEVEN:

Arrivals, Welcome and Un

Philippa touched the control. Her closet door slid shut noiselessly, leaving her staring into a floor-to-ceiling mirror. She was wearing an ice-blue one-piece swimsuit that tied over one shoulder. It was the last thing she bought before leaving Alphorion; it set off her pale cloud of hair beautifully and matched her eyes exactly, but she had bought it for a Secretariat party at which Miguel's family was expected—a week before she was arrested. Until now she had not been able to look at the suit without shuddering. Now she just felt tense and numb, and yet it seemed somehow right to wear the suit.

Her bedroom door opened to reveal her mother, her expression calm and unreadable as always. "I see there's to be a shoreline party," said Director Bidding. "Are you going with anyone?"

The announcement of the party had been attached to Philippa's personal code, but all she thought was, *So they're still reading my messages?* Out loud, she said, "No one."

Her mother tapped one shapely nail against the dresser. "Can you possibly think," her soft voice sharpened ever so slightly, "that you have *any* right to sulk over *anything?*"

"I'm not sulking," Philippa said, pulling on the tunic and lacing her sandals. "I just haven't felt well." ·

"Then consult a physician. Or, if you find Dr. Tourni's facetiousness as repellent as I do, then we will find you another physician. Have you managed to alienate Governor Matthews's son?"

Philippa put her hands on her hips. "Why do you need to know?"

Her mother ignored the question as if Philippa had not spoken. "If you have, then I will make a point of inviting Director Gavras and his son for dinner next time they come into Ambora."

"Mother," Philippa said, "William Gavras is more of a slimy PC than my cousin Geoffrey."

"I might remind you that beggars can't be choosers." The door shut.

Then Philippa, who was sixteen and collected and smart and an ex-revolutionary and better than anyone at tricking guardian robots, stuck out her tongue at the door as far as it would go. It felt wonderful.

"It's up to you, Clea," her mother said, smiling.

"Don't be a corrosive PC!" Clea's sister Andrena said passionately. "*Everyone* in my cohort with an older sister or brother is going, and if you don't let me go, then they'll all say I'm a baby, and it'll be *your fault.*"

"The invitation was for Cohort Threes and the incoming Cohort Threes," Clea's father said.

Andrena tossed her hair back, scornfully dismissing his statement as immaterial. "I happen to know," she said, "That Tris Yamoto is going."

"Ah!" Dr. Tourni said weakly. "Not quite nine, and already in love!"

"How corrosive, Mom!" Andrena made a horrible face. "Tris and the others are making a holovid, and I want to be *in* it! So, *Clea*—"

"Oh, I'll take you," Clea said. "But when I want to leave, you are to go with me without yelling like I'm torturing you."

"I'll be perfect!" Andrena promised exuberantly.

A few minutes later, the sisters were walking along the path that led to the beach. Clea knew that some of the older teens would meet at a short cut on a high cliff and rappel down, but with Andrena along, the long way had to be the only way.

As she walked, Clea realized she was not in any great hurry. She could still feel a peculiar tension deep in her brain, which indicated that all was not well with the other five members of the gang. Oblivious to this, her sister chattered happily, ". . . and Tris's brother Earl said that Mr. Oblitt, who teaches you *old* kids, and is the fastest at freeball on his old planet, also knows how to do swordfighting, just like old-time pirates, and he's teaching Tris and Tank so they can do it in the vid! And then they'll send the vid to Felicidad and make zillions and zillions of credits . . ."

"Great," Clea murmured as they rounded the last long, gentle slope and looked down at the black-sand beach below the towering cliffs. Color was scattered along the wide strip of beach: blankets and towels and umbrellas and food hampers and kids in brightly colored swimwear.

Andrena soon spotted some of her own friends, and ran down the long path to join them. Clea followed more slowly. She did not have to search for her own group. She knew where they were. Zach had called earlier, saying he'd be delayed, but the others were all there.

She kept walking, splashing her feet through the foamy water, until she saw Sean, Will, and Arkady playing some sort of game with five or six others in the shallow surge. First Sean and then Arkady sent glances toward Philippa, who was sitting alone.

Clea could *feel* that Sean was still mad. Arkady was much harder to read. Clea saw him send a long, expressionless gaze at Philippa, who was at that moment absorbed in pulling off her tunic cover.

"Hi, Clea!" Will called, his voice barely heard over the hissing seawater.

They're trying to ignore Philippa, Clea realized. *As if that will fix anything!* Clea defiantly marched right up to Philippa. "All right if I sit with you?" she asked.

Philippa's smile was wry, but all she said was, "Plenty of room."

Clea dumped her blanket down and sat down on it as Philippa pulled out a vial of cream from her bag. With a slight grimace, the Alphorionite girl uncapped the cream and began rubbing it over her skin.

"What does that feel like?" Clea asked, looking at Philippa's pale skin, which was already faintly mottled with pink in the strong sunlight.

"It feels like grease, and when sand sticks to it, it's worse. You're lucky." Philippa glanced enviously at Clea's smooth, warm brown skin.

Clea thought so, too, but she would not say such a thing out loud. Instead, she said cautiously, "Are you feeling better?"

Philippa paused for a moment, then went on rubbing the cream. "Oh. Yes. I didn't make it to the lab for the model project. How'd that go?"

"Nowhere. Other memories . . . thoughts . . . kept intruding," Clea said, hugging her knees.

Philippa capped her vial and tossed it in her bag, then turned her head to look out at the far waves. "Look. Mr. Oblitt's a better swimmer than any of them." She pointed to a dark head way out.

"Oh, Mr. Oblitt came!" Clea grinned. "Is that why they're all crowded over here?" She nodded at the girls on the lower slope. Half the girls in the Third Cohort were in love with this popular teacher.

"Yes. Much good it will do them," Philippa commented.

"He doesn't date students, that much I know."

"But he does date someone over in geophysics." Philippa gave a curious grimace, not quite a smile.

"How'd you know that?"

"Oh," Philippa said and shrugged, reaching into her bag again to pull out a cold-drink flask. "I once made the mistake of mentioning to my parents how good-looking Mr. Oblitt is. Just conversation. A few days later, mother's secretary, Hannah, took care to tell me casually that he's seeing someone."

Clea was perplexed. "Why?"

"Because, he's just a lowly teacher. *Quite* ineligible." Philippa's brows were raised high, exactly like her mother's. She offered the flask to Clea. "Want some?"

Clea shook her head, laughing. "That's ridiculous! As if we're thinking about marriage at our age!"

"On Alphorion, in the *best* society, you understand, you think about marriage as soon as a child is born."

"Yuck!" Clea gasped. "But what if your fiancé grows up into a toroid?"

Philippa's eyes were brightly ironic. "Then you develop a hobby."

"You sound like you were in that situation," Clea exclaimed, then immediately regretted saying it. Not that Philippa's face showed any emotion, but Clea felt the mental closing off, exactly as if a wall had gone up between them. She felt her cheeks get hot. "Never mind."

Philippa gave a little shrug. "As it happens, there *was* a toroid." She added thoughtfully, "He always licked his lips, and he liked to scare people's pets. Only the small pets, of course."

Clea made a face. "Sounds real hyborious."

"Oh, there were good things about Alphorion as well."

"Like that bathing suit. You sure didn't get it here."

Philippa smiled, then turned her head to watch a group of boys running toward the surf with their silanna-brown surfboards tucked under their arms. Sean, Will, and Arkady were still playing about in the shallow surf. "I don't see Zach," she murmured.

"He'll be here later. Got stuck with duty driving some visiting bigwig around, showing off the city."

Philippa's eyes were still on the boys as she said, "I'm sorry I didn't come the other day. Next time I will."

Clea hesitated. Her first impulse was to reach out,

but this cool, sophisticated girl had never shown any sign of wanting any such thing. Bravely, she said, "Philippa, if there's a problem, we're here to help."

"Help." Philippa shook her head. "Remember, I get the crazy current, too. Sean's giving me the 'you rotter' treatment, or I'll volunteer to shovel recycle slop for the next five rotations!"

Clea's arms tightened around her legs, pressing her stomach. "It's only because he does care."

Philippa gave her head a little shake, but before she could say anything, the girls saw Daphne DeVries, her long hair braided with bright yellow ribbons, walking with a new girl.

"And here are Philippa Bidding and Clea Tourni, also in our Cohort. You'll be in Clea's work detail." Daphne turned to smile at Philippa and Clea. "You don't mind my interruption? Noriko's new, and I thought I'd introduce her around a bit. Noriko Wilder."

Philippa made one of those graceful gestures that Clea wished she could pull off without looking like an idiot. Gracious and regal, but entirely natural. "Sit down and join us!"

Clea watched as Daphne promptly dropped a huge, rainbow-striped blanket down. Noriko sat with a smooth, compact movement on one edge of Daphne's blanket. She was a small girl, with a dainty build and exotic slanting dark eyes. Her face was as pretty as a doll's, but there was something about her short, black hair that hinted she was not the doll type. She was dressed plainly in an old black jumper, and as Clea watched she suddenly stood up and shucked it in a quick, efficient movement. Under it was a black one-piece suit.

Clea then realized that Noriko's eyes had been staring seaward for a long time, watching the surfers trying to ride fast-moving waves. She barely noticed Sean, Will, and Arkady, who were coming toward them.

"That. What's that called?" Noriko pointed at the surfers.

"It's called surfing," Sean said. "Hi, Daph. Who's this?"

Noriko was silent, her eyes still on the surfers.

"Her name is Noriko," Daphne said, smiling up at the boys.

"Surfing's from Old Earth," Will offered. "Twentieth century or something. We make our boards out of silanna, the same stuff as the walls and just about everything else."

"I'll try it," Noriko said.

"Uh, Gauguin's tides are strong," Will began a warning.

"Why don't you see how you do swimming in the surf," Sean said carefully. "Our tides are dangerous, like Will said."

Noriko turned her head at that. She simply looked at Sean, saying nothing, but Clea felt that look. Sean seemed to feel it as well; he stared as Noriko got up and ran lightly over the sand to where several boards lay. She picked one up and balanced it on her head. Without a backward glance, she splashed into the water.

Sean was after her at once. Will sighed, sinking down onto the sand. Arkady hesitated, his gaze moving past Clea to Philippa, who was watching Noriko and Sean. Then he ran to join the others in the water.

Clea watched, feeling such a strange melange of

emotional undercurrents that she just hugged her knees tighter. She could not repress a tiny spurt of triumph at the way Philippa was staring at Sean; Philippa must have felt that sudden electricity between Noriko and Sean just as strongly as she had. But then Clea noticed something that made all her usual problems go out of her head.

Daphne was also staring after the boys, her pretty profile somber.

Oh, no. I hadn't even thought of Daphne liking Sean, too. What a great bunch we are. Clea buried her forehead on her knees, trying not to laugh suddenly.

"Whoops, down she goes!" Will said. "Oh! She's going out again!"

"Looks like Sean's trying to talk her out of it," came Philippa's cool voice. "That'll keep her at it if anything will."

"Aw, Sean's all right. He just worries about us. Can't help it. Comes with the territory—his dad and all," Will said. "He wouldn't let me try today. It's too rough, but maybe later." he added with a sigh. "So! You girls going to the dance?" Philippa shrugged.

"Well, of course," Daphne said brightly. "Comes with *my* father's territory, you might say—"

"Daphne!" A shout from behind interrupted.

Clea saw Zach's young brother Tris hovering anxiously just on the other side of the promontory. As Daphne looked up, Tris motioned at her excitedly. Daphne got up and walked toward him, and was soon surrounded by Tris's gang of movie moguls. Paul and Tris both began talking at once, then Tris laughed and ran off with the rest of his gang.

"Paul knows *her?*" Clea heard Will mutter.

Paul had lingered, his hands picking absently at the terminal tucked tightly under his arm. For a moment they stood there, the graceful, tall girl talking with the boy nearly half a head shorter and almost two years younger. Then Daphne nodded and smiled, obviously concluding the subject, but as she turned to rejoin the group, Clea saw Paul following slowly.

"Hyborious!" Will said suddenly, squinting out at the faraway figures on the sea. "She's staying up! Not too bad for one day's work!" Will grinned. "Anyway, as I was saying, there's that dance tomorrow night. Seems to me that you're fairly new yourself, Daphne. Could be you might want to go with an oldie."

"Ouch," said Philippa, staring out to sea. "That was one hard fall!"

"New girl down?" Will asked.

"No, Sean!" Philippa said with a grim smile.

"Well, he's going out again." Will turned back.

Clea looked at Daphne, and saw to her surprise that the redhead's cheeks were flushed with what was clearly anger. Just then Paul leaned close and whispered something to her, and she said, "Why, Paul, how *gallant!* And *thoughtful!* I'd love to!"

Paul moved back and disappeared, stumbling, over the sandy hill, looking as if he'd been struck by a hoversled. Clea watched in blank surprise as Daphne then propped her chin on one slim hand, and glared with a dangerous smile at Will. "You were saying, o great oldie? A crust about to be thrown?"

"C-crust?" Will repeated.

Uh-oh, Clea thought. *She thinks he's being condescending, but doesn't realize that's just Will being awkward and klutzy, because he thinks he's a klutz.*

"Just wanted to invite you to the dance," he went on.

"Sorry!" Daphne tossed her head. "I fear I'm previously engaged." And as Will stared, Daphne put her sunhat on and stood up. "I think I'll start a new fashion. Dating younger men—they're so much more mature, don't you think?" She walked briskly toward some other classmates.

Is that because she doesn't think he's a klutz? Great going, Clea. Sort out everyone else's business, your own being so perfect. Her thoughts were interrupted by the sudden sound of hard breathing.

Zach ran up, his long hair flying in the breeze. There was an unfamiliar serious look to his eyes that made Clea's insides go cold.

"Philippa." He dropped to her blanket. "I got away when I could. Seems this Planetary League pal of my dad's isn't here on vacation, but some sort of duty, and that," he paused to catch his breath, "seems to include wanting to talk to you."

TWELVE:

Is This a Conspiracy?

Clea's amazement at Zach's news was nothing compared to her reaction to what Philippa then said: "Here we go again."

Two shadows loomed over Clea's shoulder as Arkady and Sean emerged from the water. Sean absentmindedly grabbed Will's towel. Arkady shook himself, sending drops of water flying off.

"Planetary League officer wants to talk to Philippa. I heard it purely by accident," Zach said. "Came down as soon as I could."

Philippa had been staring at her hands since her one comment. Now she looked up as Sean knelt directly in front of her. "Want us to help or do you want us out? You've got to tell us now."

There was a silence that seemed hours long to Clea. She was vaguely aware of the sea's crashing and hissing, and the voices of other kids talking and laughing, but all those things seemed far away.

When Philippa spoke, Clea almost could not hear it. "Why?"

Sean hesitated, and Zach smiled at Philippa. "Would you help one of us if we were in trouble?"

Philippa looked surprised. "Of course," she said instantly.

"Well then."

"But none of you would ever—" She made a gesture and shook her head.

"Have you done something truly unforgivable?" Clea heard herself posing one of her father's Concerned Dad Conversation Openers.

"Not to me. To my parents—"

"Then that settles it!" Sean said, giving Philippa a conspiratorial wink.

Philippa took a deep, shaky breath. "I—you don't know about what happened on Alphorion?" She glanced at Arkady, who was still standing with his arms folded. She met a cool, blank stare and her cheeks turned faintly pink. "Okay. You don't know." Briefly, she described her career as a Leffie, and the result. "So I came here and meant to start over. But the other day, when I got a message from Miguel, I—I had to find out what he wanted. He needed a place to hide, so I brought him from Gandria. He's in the retreat house by the sea. He's going to try to get back to Alphorion somehow. That officer must be here to ask me about him."

Arkady spoke. "We'll get him."

Sean nodded up at Arkady. "Right." He turned to Philippa. "How's this for a plan? You hold off the League officer as long as you can until we can get your friend out of that house. This way, when you do have your interview, if you don't know where Miguel is, then you can't say where he is."

Philippa's smile was a bit uncertain. "I don't know how to thank you."

"Don't," Arkady said.

Sean grinned, tossing down Will's towel. "And if you *ever* assume *we'd* treat you like that bunch of toroids on your old planet did, then—"

"Get your dad to put her in Santori's office as filing assistant for a year's jug time," Zach suggested when Sean hesitated.

There was a general groan at the unpopular assistant director's name, and Arkady and Sean grabbed their belongings.

"You'll have to use a code," Philippa said. "Or he might not believe you. Tell him that I'm sending the Dickens spool. For the literature class."

Sean gave a nod and he and Arkady sauntered away. They waved at a few friends and exchanged greetings once or twice, but nothing stopped their progress across the sand, and they were soon gone from view.

Zach shook his head admiringly, his smile more lopsided than ever. "Thinks fast, our Sean."

"That he does," Will agreed. "So now what?"

Zach ran his hand through his hair. "Well, seems to me what you've got to do, Pippa, is stay away from home for a while. The message will go there, and if you're not there to get it . . . that buys you some time."

"But won't they come looking for me?" Philippa asked quietly.

"No. You're not under arrest; you haven't done anything. They don't like to attract a lot of attention when they just want to talk to someone, and sending people to search all over would do just that."

Clea said, "How about if you come home with me

after the party, and we'll send a message to your home just before we go out to eat—"

"*And* see a vid," Will put in.

"Exactly! And later we'll send another message that you're spending the night with me. But we'll be gone *early* tomorrow, so they can't reach us then."

"I'll hang out at home in case anyone needs messages relayed," Zach volunteered.

"Whatever happens, I want you all to know this means a lot," Philippa said.

Zach winked. "Just remember a year's jug time with Mr. Santori's happy smile, and trust us next time. Copy?"

"Copy," said Philippa.

Paul felt tall and strong and debonair.

He glanced back, seeing Daphne's bright hair with its yellow ribbons as she talked with a group of kids her own age. "She said yes," he breathed. He felt like ten thousand kilowatts of electricity.

"There you are," Tris called impatiently. "Come on, we're waiting!"

Paul sauntered down the dune to join the group. Their secret vid project seemed babyish and trivial compared to Love between Man and Woman, but he had agreed . . . and they could certainly benefit from a mature point of view.

"So we're set then," Tris began. "Daphne says we can get a handcam and vidtape for sunlight shooting, so let's set our schedule now."

Paul pulled his terminal from under his arm, and hastily set up columns. "Now," he said. "I'll list your names, your school, and Community Service schedules, and you can tape the scenes involving those of you with matching free periods—"

Tank shook his head. "That'll be a mess. Go through the story from beginning to end. Then it'll make sense to us."

Paul snorted with impatience. "That's a waste of time! It'll be much more efficient if you use your people as they are available. As for that story, it's not going to make any more sense if you start at the end and tape backwards."

"You think our story is a mess?" Mik demanded.

"I've *offered* to help you with the logical and historical inconsistencies," Paul said. "As for the schedule, just do this—"

"Why don't you go on home and let us work out our schedule," Tris cut in coldly.

Paul looked at Tris, whose brown eyes were less friendly than he'd ever seen. He looked around in growing surprise, seeing that the others were not only angry but offended. "But you wanted—" he began.

No one said anything.

Trying to maintain a dignified expression, Paul walked away. "Immature," he muttered not quite under his breath. He knew he was right, but still he felt deflated as he started toward home.

The golden afternoon rays were beginning to slant across the tops of the waves when several locos arrived, summoning home the younger kids. Twilight on Gauguin lasted a long time, but the tide would soon be coming in.

Clea, shaking the sand from her towel, watched the new girl Noriko ride one last huge wave in, then disappear in the crashing white foam. A moment later, she was walking up the beach to hand the borrowed board back to Will.

Clea thought about that moment between Noriko and Sean. It had definitely been charged, and it made her uncomfortable to realize how clearly she'd felt it. She wasn't going out with Sean anymore, and yet the current was still connecting them.

"Maybe we'd best leave." Will's voice broke into her thoughts. Clea looked up, glad to be distracted. "I'll go find my sister," she said, and started down the beach. "Meet you all at the path." She walked a few steps, then noticed that she had company. Looking up she saw Zach smiling his lopsided smile. She grinned at him. One thing about Zach: he was always comfortable to be around.

"I think I'll offer some lessons," he said, thoughtfully.

"Lessons? What, surfing?" Clea asked, scanning the tangle of smaller kids playing in the shallow surge.

"Lessons in what they call shielding."

Clea forgot about Andrena, and studied Zach. "Shielding, as in empathic shielding?" she asked warily.

"Yeah. My mother's been drilling me. I haven't told her why, but this is one jug duty I've actually worked hard at."

Clea nodded slowly. Being from Galahad, she was used to this kind of talk; when she'd first arrived on Gauguin, she'd had to get over feeling isolated among people who could not read her moods. Now she realized that she had gotten used to that. *You're busy reading them,* she thought, *forgetting that maybe they can read you.* She looked away, embarrassed. Was Zach hinting at her own problems?

Zach said reflectively, "You might have noticed that the general energy level rose about five notches when Noriko met our Sean."

Clea laughed a little breathlessly.

"And it got me to thinking. Maybe I should pass on a few of my mother's lessons. Or else we might all end up watching one another's dates."

Clea laughed a little shakily. "I'm glad I'm not the only one who felt it. You're right—this could get embarrassing. Do you know enough to teach us shielding?"

"I can try." Zach squinted down the beach. "There's the mid-level Tourni, and she seems to be squabbling with one mid-level Yamoto." Zach waved lazily at a dozen or so younger kids who were standing in a knot, arguing loudly. "Tris usually doesn't cause fights—outside of home."

"Andrena wants to get into his vid." Clea laughed.

"Vid? What vid?"

"A secret project that all the lower cohorts seem to know about."

Zach whistled. He said nothing, however, as they reached the kids. At the sight of two older teens, the entire group shut up in a way that would have inspired immediate suspicion, but Clea just pulled her loudly protesting sister away, and helped her gather her belongings.

Later that afternoon, Philippa silently followed Clea into the Tourni dome.

Clea realized that, though she and Philippa had known each other for months, she had only been inside Philippa's home once, and Philippa had never been in hers.

As Clea stepped inside, she looked around as if

seeing her home for the first time. Familiar furniture now defined itself as shabby, unmatched pieces from the old home; the vidscreen was playing some kiddie program, and Sara and Lilith Yamoto were shrieking happily, spilling some kind of crispy snack all over the floor. The door to the study was open, and inside, Clea's father was lying on the couch with a headset on, typing on a portable terminal propped on his lap, and wiggling his toes in time to some unheard music. Clea felt faintly embarrassed that the perfect Philippa was seeing her personal life. What would she think?

Clea slapped the door control, and they moved into her room. "Sorry about the mess," she said as she flopped onto her bed. "It's always chaos here on freedays—"

Philippa was still standing in the middle of the room, holding her arms just above the elbows, as if she felt cold. "It's all right," she said with a slight smile. "I like it."

"Like a curiosity exhibit?" Clea dumped out her bag.

"It's welcome. I guess that's enough of a curiosity."

Clea thought of Philippa's beautiful, spacious dome up there on Admin Hill near all the high-ranking people of Ambora—including the Matthews. She'd been there just once, when Philippa had hosted an afternoon party for her classmates. Clea wore her very best dress, and didn't recognize any of the food served, though supposedly they all had access to the same ration cards. Philippa was dressed in something pale yellow and dreamy-looking, and her gorgeous mother had walked through, shaking hands and smiling at everyone before disappearing again. An elegant party in every way, but Clea's private judgment had been "Not Fun."

Clea sighed. "What do you mean?"

Philippa turned her gem-blue eyes on her. "I'd like to come home and feel welcome," she said.

It was a simple statement, made in an unemotional tone. Clea looked back, not knowing what to say. "Well, you're welcome here," she said sincerely. "Come on. Let's flip for who gets the bathroom first."

By the time Paul got home, his mood had changed again. He had begun by thinking about actually being *alone* with Daphne, just the two of them, until they arrived at the dance. And then . . .

And then—I don't know how to dance, he realized. Also, it occurred to his usually well-ordered mind that the logistics of getting to the dance would pose problems. *Do I just meet her at her house and walk over? What if she wants to go somewhere before or after? How do I then secure transportation, when my mother and stepfather will want to go to the big parties being held in the Admin conference rooms, and what if Will also has a date?*

From there, it was easy to progress to the little details. Would she expect him to hold her hand? He wanted to hold her hand (he wanted very much to hold her hand)—but what if it was not correct to do so until a certain point during the date?

Paul groaned. "What an impossible social system," he muttered. But then he heard the front door, and he charged out of the bedroom.

"Will," he said in relief.

Will looked up, his expression slightly wary.

"I need to ask you something," Paul said.

"Now?" Will asked, indicating his sandy clothes and his beach gear still in his hand.

Paul just nodded violently, knowing he would not be able to fortify himself for these questions another time.

Will followed Paul into the room they had to share. "Line open," Will said after a long pause.

"I have a date," Paul said. He expected some kind of reaction. Surprise or even laughter, though Will had never been the type to laugh at people, but instead, Will seemed to look inward for a time.

"Date. I copy so far," Will said finally. "And you're asking me—"

"What I have to do," Paul said, feeling the urge for the first time in eight years to bite his nails.

Will sighed, short and sharp, a coming-to-a-decision sound. "Okay. Here's the data. If you did the asking, you are expected to provide the transportation to and from. If you include food in the invitation, then you provide it. If she asked you out, then it's up to her to provide this stuff."

"But what . . ." Paul grimaced, biting his thumbnail. "What about the *rest*?"

"As for what goes on during the date, you just—try to have a good time."

"Good time. Copy," Paul said. He thought of Daphne's clear gray eyes, her delightful smile, the way she walked, and the pink curve of her lips. "I think," he added as Will disappeared into the bathroom.

THIRTEEN:

Night Secrets

As soon as the powerful hovercraft was out of sight of the city, Sean's palm came down flat on the speed control. The engine obediently cranked up until they were skimming past the grassy cliffs.

The boys had barely spoken during the run from the beach to the Matthews' house where they borrowed the hovercraft. Arkady called his parents while Sean talked to his, each asking if he could stay at the other's for the night, and knowing that if they got back early, they would sleep over at Zach's. The Yamotos would never notice a couple of extra bodies.

At first, Arkady had said nothing as Sean drove northward. Now he said, "You're still angry."

"Aren't you?" Sean leaned back, his hands loose on the driving controls. A glance over at his friend showed what he'd expected: Arkady was sitting straight-backed and blank-faced, watching the road.

"The night of the storm she told me a little," Arkady said. "Not even as much as we heard today. But enough so I knew she'd been in trouble with the government on Alphorion." He hesitated a moment, as if unsure of how much to reveal. "We were trapped on that cliff. Tide was rising, and we expected to go out with a big one any moment. When she finished, she said, 'At least I won't be messing up people's lives anymore.'"

Sean snorted, swerving tightly around a group of majestic, dark-leaved vellkul trees. "Sounds like a vid."

Arkady gave him a faint smile. "Maybe you had to have been there."

Sean laughed at that, then said, "We're a team. Maybe we didn't choose to be a team, but the six of us *are* one."

"Right," Arkady agreed. "So we help her even if she's acting like a bad vid."

Sean gave him an exasperated look. "Well, we can't leave her stranded. I mean, I can't help feeling that that vision has some kind of importance. Not just for us. Importance to the colony here. And we're never going to figure out exactly what we saw, or how to convince anyone we saw it if we don't all work together. The question is, does Philippa want to work with us?"

"It looks that way."

"It does?"

Sean drove for a time in silence, turning off into mountains before Arkady replied. "Look," he said at last, "the guy's up here, but she's not with him. He's going to leave—and she's not going with him.

Whatever she was in it for when she was on Alphorion, it isn't working for her now. Maybe she wants to be one of us, but doesn't know how to say it or do it."

Sean thought that over, then smiled at his friend. "For someone who doesn't say much, you get a lot said."

"Sometimes," Arkady said.

Philippa had only brought beach things in her bag, so Clea had to loan her something to wear. Philippa accepted the first thing Clea offered her, which was one of her best outfits, expressed her thanks, and dressed without giving more than a perfunctory glance at the mirror. Still, Clea was having a hard time. The two girls were about the same height, and both had slim builds, but where Clea was skinny from neck to feet, Philippa had slender hands and legs, and gorgeous curves in between.

Clea sighed.

"Something wrong?" Philippa asked.

"Just genes," Clea grinned. "Let me send the message to your place, tell my dad we're going out, and we can leave."

They were soon walking along the pathway to city center. "I told my dad I wasn't sure when we'd be back, except late," Clea said. "I was even more vague to your parents. I hope that won't make them worry."

"They won't," Philippa assured her. "I'm completely free to jump off a volcano—the sooner the better."

"*No* rules? Even when you were out with—well, dating?"

"No rules," Philippa said with an ironic smile.

"But I did hear faint approval when I was with a parentally inspected and approved specimen."

"Such as a governor's son?" Clea couldn't help but laugh. Then she said slowly, "I don't think there's much that my parents would consider forever unforgivable." To herself, she added, *Not that I'd ever think of anything as cosmic as joining a revolution, anyway. Even Philippa's mistakes are spectacular.* "Shall we wander over to the vid center and see what the choices are, or shall we get something to eat first?"

"Thought about what we'll do with this Miguel?" Arkady asked.

"Have been thinking about it," Sean grinned. "Here's what I suggest: If he's all right we'll take him back to town and see if we can do anything for him through Transport. But if he's a stone, then let's dump him in Gandria where he first waltzed back into Miss Bidding's life." Sean was only half serious, but to his surprise, Arkady nodded acceptance.

"You got enough power to get to Gandria and back?"

Sean laughed, glancing at the course indicator. "Five klicks to go."

Sean and Arkady drove toward a spectacular sunset. The entire ocean horizon seemed to be on fire. The sun sat just above the sea, crowned by a glory of yellow, rose, apricot, and cerulean clouds.

Neither boy, however, spared the view more than a glance. Their eyes were on the dark, still house before them.

Sean slowed the hovercraft, and allowed it to settle gently on its pads before he took his hands from the controls. "You know," he said with a slight grin, "this might sound stupid, but we forgot to ask Philippa if the guy is armed."

"She might not know," Arkady's answer came in the gathering gloom.

The boys got out of the scooter and walked slowly toward the house. They stopped when they were in range of the intercom system. Sean spoke. "Miguel. Philippa said to tell you that she's sending the Dickens spool. For the literature class." He felt silly saying such a thing, then reminded himself that it would feel a whole lot worse if Miguel was armed and didn't want company.

The door opened, and a tall figure came out and stood on the threshold. "Where is she?" came a deep voice.

"Safe. But the father of someone in our group is a retired P.L. commander, being visited by an old friend," Arkady said calmly. "Wants to talk to Philippa. We're here to see that Philippa has no current news."

There was a hesitation, then: "Your group?"

"Friends," Sean said.

Miguel stepped down suddenly. Sean found himself looking up into the face of a black-haired and green-eyed young man some years older than himself. Miguel was studying him as closely, he realized, as Arkady went on, "If we can take you somewhere, it might solve Philippa's problem, and ours, and maybe yours."

Miguel said, "I'd intended to leave by tomorrow. Help me check the house for signs of my presence, then we can depart when you wish."

Sean and Arkady followed Miguel in silence. Sean felt strange, poking around a house he'd never seen before. He heard Arkady's low voice once or twice, and Miguel's quick response as they adjusted furniture or picked up a thread from the carpet. Sean's mind was still busy with his first sight of Miguel's face.

He'd felt a jolt when he realized Miguel's features were vaguely familiar. *I've seen 'em in the mirror once or twice. Is that why she dated me, as a kind of stand-in for this Alphorionite revolutionary? What an inspiring thought!* Sean poked at the kitchen setup, torn between irritation with Philippa, irritation with this Miguel character, and a strong desire to laugh. His attention was reclaimed by Arkady's voice, apparently answering a question.

"We don't really know what it is that you've done. We're up here to do what we can to keep her from being arrested a second time." Arkady paused, then added, "Arrested and deserted."

Miguel looked up from replacing the communications console cover. "I'm sorry she still feels that way," he said.

Arkady did not answer.

Sean said reluctantly, "We don't know that she does. She hasn't said much. But she doesn't trust much either."

Miguel clicked the cover into place. "Being arrested as a Leffie did not completely change her," he said finally.

Sean thought of Philippa's smooth, handsome parents. He remembered his mother's laughing voice in the car the other night, and knew that Miguel was right. He looked over at Arkady and saw the Thetan's eyes flick briefly southward.

"If you're ready," Sean said, "we can get you into Ambora and see what's going on at Transport."

"I thank you," Miguel said.

They carefully closed the house up, then climbed into the hovercraft.

The theater was completely dark, of course, but Clea knew that Philippa was not really paying much attention to the holovid. Maybe it was the way her breathing stayed steady and controlled. On her other side, Will huffed with quiet laughter at the funny parts, and went absolutely still during the chases. Ordinarily, Clea liked adventure vids, but it was hard to get into the story and believe in the problems of the gorgeous heroine and handsome hero when, in real life, there was a gorgeous friend and a handsome and heroic ex-boyfriend who were having problems of their own.

Suddenly Clea could *feel* Philippa's inner tension, like boiling lava in the pit of her stomach. Clea forced her mind back to the vid. *Zach's right. It's too hard to turn the current off when we don't want it.* She was glad when the vid was finally over.

Both moons were up when they left the theater, and the air was cool and breezy on the skywalk. Will cracked some jokes as they strolled along. Next to Clea, Philippa walked slowly, her eyes on the moonlit waterfall. Her pale hair blowing about her face looked ghostly.

Clea rubbed her arms. "It's chilly. Is the season changing?"

"Rain soon," Will said. "My father says the animals are living near water areas now, and the grasses are dying."

"Sean and Arkady are driving fast," Philippa said softly. "But they're not safe yet."

"What?" Will asked. "I feel them moving, if I

think about them, but I don't sense danger."

"Neither do I," Clea said, though she shivered again. *I really hate this. I get scared so easily.* "Maybe I'd better call home. I could get my mom or dad to send a message to your parents about your spending the night. Then neither of us have to talk to them."

Philippa smiled. "For someone who doesn't like getting in trouble, you're showing real promise."

Sean's hovercraft raced eastward in the deepening twilight.

"How'd you get on the planet?" Sean glanced back at Miguel. In the backseat darkness, the whites of Miguel's eyes glowed green like Philippa's. It bothered Sean, so he looked away again.

"False ID," Miguel's quiet voice came out of the gloom.

"Can you not reuse it?" Arkady asked.

"It was traced. They seem to know I landed here."

"You've been monitoring the bands?"

"Yes."

"Then there might be a problem getting you out again."

"Set me near your spaceport, and you've saved me a long walk."

Sean glanced over at Arkady. The Thetan's face was barely discernable in the reflected glow of the instrument panel, but it seemed as expressionless as usual. Sean remembered the mental link, and tried thinking a query at Arkady. Nothing: he already knew that Arkady was sitting beside him, and anything beyond that was as blank as Arkady's expression.

Belatedly, Sean realized that that was usual with Arkady. He couldn't remember anyone talking about getting emotional current from Arkady any more than they had from Philippa. *How do they cut themselves out?* he wondered. He knew that he projected very clearly; there'd been plentiful commentary about the state of his temper lately, from Zach and . . . and Clea, though her comments had a different perspective. Sean grimaced at the dark landscape sliding by. What a mess this craziness made in an already crazy life!

Arkady's voice broke into his thoughts. "Taking the long route?"

"Thought I'd better," Sean answered, glad to have an excuse to stop thinking about Clea, and how he'd messed up *that* relationship. "Everyone knows the governor's car, and I don't need a zillion questions tomorrow from someone who might see us pass through the center of Ambora."

"Making good speed," Arkady said approvingly.

"Yep." Sean grinned. "While I couldn't drive it, I thought I might as well modify it a little. Wired around the regulator, in case we need full power and can't stop to mess with the navpack."

"Set the shorting bars in, so you won't burn the engine out?"

"Yep. Ran three or four tests on scoots at the yard—"

"High step," Miguel cut in sharply. "*Jump!*"

Sean's mind squawked, *What?* as his fingers swiped the toggle he'd just shown Arkady, and his other hand increased the pressor beam to maximum.

The hoverscooter bounced high in the air—and a vehicle passed beneath them at screaming speed.

"Did you feel that?" Philippa asked sharply just as Clea's cold fingers groped toward her hand.

"They're in danger," Clea whispered, sensing a sudden, strong tension from Sean. She shivered. "This is so weird!"

"We'd better get to your house, in case Zach calls," Philippa said. "We might be needed to help." She sprinted across the bridge and up the pathway, with Clea laboring to catch up. For a time, Will's long legs kept him in pace, but soon his steps flagged. Defeated by gravity, he walked as fast as he could toward his own home as the girls disappeared into the dark night.

"They tried to ram us." Arkady's face was pressed to his window.

Sean glanced back at Miguel, and saw the steady glow of those green eyes. "Did you—?"

"No one but Philippa knows I'm here. And maybe the P.L. They'd stop us, not try to ram us. I got a glimpse of that craft: Old cross-country model, ID panel blanked," Miguel said shortly.

"Maybe our beam pressing them down gave 'em something to think about," Sean muttered. The hoverscooter was in low-step mode again, skimming just inches above the road, and Sean increased his speed. The path wound along the top of the hills behind Ambora, which was not the sort of terrain he liked speeding across at night. His hands were light on the controls, though, in case—

"He's here," Miguel said. "On the left—"

"Cliff ahead!" Arkady pointed at the orange indicators.

They're lying in wait! In less than a second, a plan formed in Sean's mind. He acted on it before there was time to consider whether it would work or not.

He spotted the attacker's twin lights coming fast at the angle Miguel had indicated. When the other vehicle was about to hit them, he veered, jumped his craft, and drove straight for the cliff. At the last possible second, he cut the lights and threw them into a swerve that sent them angling in a U up and down a rocky cliff.

There was a nightmarish wrestle with the speeding hovercraft over rough ground, then he brought them to a crashing stop in a thick grove of trees.

And, at last, he took a breath.

FOURTEEN:

Private Interview

Arkady said, "Maybe he'll think we went off the cliff."

"That was the idea," Sean said. "I jumped us so our beam would hit him, making him think there was some kind of impact. He's faster—we can't outrun him. But who is he?"

"And what's he up to?" Arkady shook his head. "This is another one. We can't report it because we can't explain why we were here, and we can't produce even a description of a culprit."

Sean slammed his hand on the console. "But we can't leave, either—what if he's back up on the road, waiting?"

"We're hidden here. I suggest we wait till daylight," Arkady said.

"Unless he has infrared," Miguel put in.

"He'd see this hot engine a mile away—" Sean started.

Arkady said dispassionately, "No. Or he would have cut his lights the second time, at least."

"Right," Miguel agreed calmly.

They sounded matter-of-fact. Sean wondered if he was the only one with a pounding heart, trying to choke its way into his neck. He snorted a laugh. "This is what, my second day with driving privileges back? If I trash this barrel, it's going to be a long career on foot."

Clea closed the door as Philippa's fingers tapped out Zach's code.

Zach must have been waiting right by his comm-link. His face came on screen immediately. He looked uncharacteristically somber to Philippa.

Clea's voice was high and nervous. "Something's happened!"

Zach nodded somewhat distractedly, then shot them a quick grin. "Hold on. Great when your dad runs the comm-link system—ah! There's Will on the other screen. What's that, Will? No, I haven't got any messages from Sean and Arkady—just felt something happen!"

Philippa watched Zach's face as the familiar brown eyes focused away for a few seconds. Then Zach was back with the girls, his voice low. "Sean and Arkady are covered for tonight, I found out. Will suggests we plan for tomorrow, in case we have to cover them."

"Both Sean and Arkady have jug with me at the repair yard," Philippa said. "I can make up some story—"

Zach gave her a warning glance. "You'd do best to look clean, in case you get your League visitor."

"I'm drudging at the Power Dome," Clea said worriedly. "How can I—"

Zach winked. "All right. It's up to Master-Plan Yamoto, I can see. I'm up for jug with my mother, so I'll put in calls that they've been co-opted into an experiment with us. Also, an early breakfast invite."

Clea said, "But what if they're gone all day?"

"We'll be in touch all day. School at midshift shouldn't be hard. Oblitt won't ask too many questions—"

"And they have study time at late shift with me," Philippa said.

"Then just maybe we can pull this thing off." Zach smiled brightly.

Philippa smiled back. *So you say, but you're thinking: What will happen when that P.L. officer does catch up with me? Will I pull you in after me?* Out loud, she said, "So all that's left is, who will get the first dance tomorrow night?"

"Hey!" Zach's brown eyes widened. "Maybe we can waylay old Sean and Arkady for another night, leaving me a harem!"

Philippa cut the line on him.

Clea turned to her, smiling nervously. "It's going to be a long night, I suspect. Maybe we should try to sleep."

Philippa glanced at the still-blinking message light. Clea noticed it and hesitated. "Oh. Do you think we should—"

Philippa's finger touched the delete button. "Oops. My mistake."

Clea sighed. "Will your parents be very angry?"

"I'm sure they are now," Philippa said as the girls went back through the dark dome to the bedroom.

"Maybe I'll get lucky and they'll never speak to me again."

"Real hyborious," Arkady heard Sean say as he shifted position again. "Cold out, but can't risk heat. No weapons, so we can't go scouting. Left the rest of our lunch behind so as not to make a mess in the craft. Still in beach clothes, and this sand I'm sitting on feels just great."

"I brought an emergency ration from the house," Miguel spoke from the darkness in the back seat. There was a faint crackle of plastic wrap, and Arkady felt something touch his shoulder. He reached, and his fingers closed on a square of soft food. He took a bite, not caring what it was.

"Well, life's better," Sean said after a moment. "Food does that. You wouldn't also happen to have a Standard League-issue stungun on hand?"

Miguel laughed quietly. "No stungun. If our visitors come knocking on the door, these seat supports make serviceable clubs. Then, if you want more power, there are some things you can do to the engine."

Thus answering two questions about Miguel. No, he's not armed, but yes, Philippa's idealistic revolutionary has seen action. I wonder if she knows that? Arkady did not voice his thought. He said only, "Shall we set watch periods?"

"You're not sleeping." Clea rolled over and peered through the darkness at the form on the bed. "Worried?"

"And thinking," Philippa's soft whisper came back.

"If it would help to talk . . ." Clea leaned her head on her hand.

"Someday, perhaps." Philippa's voice was very low. Clea heard a friendly tone next: "That's not a habit I ever learned."

"What did your friends talk about?" Clea asked, curious.

"Events. Vids and plays and music. Other people—seldom good, that! You learn early that sharing your thoughts is to put weapons into others' hands. I knew how to hide my thoughts by the time I was six, about the time I first went to society parties."

Clea shivered. "It's true you don't want everyone to know what's in your mind. But hiding your true self from your *friends!* How awful!"

"Depends on what you're used to. For me, sharing inner thoughts feels too much like my skin's off."

"I'm sorry. I'm prying," Clea said contritely.

"Not that." Philippa's voice still sounded warm. "I like your idea of friendship, but it may take me a while to get used to it."

At first, none of them slept.

After a long silence, Miguel asked some easy questions about the colony. Sean described what a new city being built was like, and added at Miguel's encouragement a description of how they nearly lost the colony in the ion storm. Miguel asked about silanna, and wanted to know what an earthquake felt like. All easy questions. Sean talked, mostly, with a few words put in from time to time by Arkady.

He hasn't asked our names, Sean realized after a time. *In case he gets caught?*

He also realized that Philippa's name had not come up again. Sean wondered if that related to Arkady's silence for so long, and terseness whenever he did speak. *Arkady doesn't trust this guy, either, for reasons relating to his escape from Alphorion, or maybe because he doesn't trust what he might hear about Philippa.*

Sean repressed a sigh, trying for the hundredth time to get comfortable in the driver's seat. Much to his surprise, he dozed; when he opened his eyes, weak light gleamed through the dark, smooth branches of a huge vellkul tree.

Clea and Philippa rose at dawn, before anyone else in the Tourni family was stirring. They dressed hurriedly, and decided to breakfast somewhere in city center before Philippa went out to the repair yard.

Outside, a loco sat gleaming on the pathway. "Good morning, dear Philippa," it began. "Your father will be here soon to give you a ride." Then it glided away silently.

Philippa stared after it, saying, "Hmm! I didn't know they could get it to do that."

"What? Oh, your parents?" Clea felt her heart beating faster. She hadn't expected them to be caught so soon.

Philippa smiled calmly, but Clea noticed that her face seemed more pale than usual in the early morning light. "Let's go anyway."

The girls walked fast in the chilly air. As they reached the pathway that ran along the river, the glowglobes winked out. A new day.

When the hoverscooter came up behind them, it

was quite sudden. They heard the quiet hiss of its pressor beam, then suddenly it was there. The passenger door sprang open. Clea glanced in and saw Philippa's father, large and unsmiling, sitting at the controls. "Good morning, Philippa," he said pleasantly. "Good morning, Miss Tourni. Philippa, you have an appointment. Shall I convey you anywhere, Miss Tourni?"

"No—yes." Clea first backed away, finding that pleasant, polite voice frightening in its ordinariness. Anger or threats would somehow be less sinister. She wanted to run, but then she realized she'd be deserting Philippa. Swallowing with a dry throat, she said, "I have no plans, Philippa, if you'd like—"

"It's all right." Philippa gave her a brief smile. "Why don't you work ahead on the assignment? I'll catch up to you when this is over."

"If that's what you want," Clea said slowly.

"Bye." Philippa climbed into the car, settled her bag on her lap, and the door shut.

Clea watched the hovercraft hiss quietly up the street. She waited until it was out of sight, then began to run.

Sean stared at the dead control panel. He tried once again to start the engine: nothing.

"Rot-reeking, night-crawling . . ." He muttered curses in five Earth languages as he slammed out and opened the navpack. Soon the three of them were dismantling the engine to find out what had jolted loose, or broken, during the crash landing the night before. "What am I going to say to my father this time?" Sean muttered, setting aside a casing. "Miguel, you Leffie characters need a driver?"

Philippa rubbed her eyes and took a slow breath. *One good thing,* she thought as her father parked the scooter in his reserved place in the Admin lot. *I don't have to close out the others anymore.*

She didn't think about the ice-cold silence during the ride, or her father's soft, "I will talk to you when your interview is done."

They walked side by side without speaking. This wing of the Admin Dome was unfamiliar to Philippa; the person behind the desk wore a neat blue uniform with a Planetary League insignia. "Miss Bidding? Commander Archetraev will see you shortly. Please follow me."

Her father started to follow as well, and Philippa almost smiled when the man said firmly but politely, "The commander asked to see Miss Bidding, Director."

The door closed behind them. Philippa braced herself.

A short hall led into a small room. And there, instead of a twin to the tall, sarcastic investigator she had faced on Alphorion, she saw a short, trim woman who looked about the same age as Commander Yamoto.

Unthreatening brown eyes studied her, and the commander said in a mild voice, "Please sit down, Miss Bidding. I asked for this interview early so I would not disturb your studies. It should not take much of your time."

Philippa sat down and folded her hands in her lap. "What can I do for you?" She smiled her best society smile.

"Miss Bidding, I am aware of the circumstances that led to your family's relocation on this planet. I understand that you were arrested for participation in an illegal organization, and had you been of age, you would have been tried and convicted. I also gather that your sentiments about this group and its goals underwent no change during the time you spent with the Youth Authority."

The commander paused and looked up expectantly, reminding Philippa suddenly of a bird waiting for a crumb.

"Well, they didn't try very hard," Philippa said.

"I understand that no information of value was obtained from you."

"I didn't know any." Philippa shrugged. "Everyone had code names."

"They seem to have dropped the code names since then." The commander's eyes crinkled. "Your name came up recently, in connection with a cell operating in the capital. You were identified as a former member." She was serious now. "One of your ex-colleagues participated in the cell's recent attack on a communications installation on Arlicot Island. He was shaken considerably by the violence of this attack; several communications personnel died, in addition to half of a group of tourists from New Olirood Settlement who chanced to be viewing the facility that day. Twenty-four people died altogether, and forty were seriously injured."

Philippa felt sick inside. "Our cell did not believe in violent acts to win our goal," she said. "It must have been some other Leffie group." *If what you say is even true.*

"It was the cell led by Alynn Tolivier and Miguel Arcaro," the commander responded. "They had apparently agreed to act with a north-city cell, led by a couple named Sigall. The idea was to take over the communications center and force negotiations, but the play of events very quickly got beyond the control of Arcaro and Tolivier."

So that's why Carl Albertin betrayed them. He probably felt betrayed when innocent people died.

If it happened.

Philippa rubbed her eyes, trying to think fast. Somehow, this felt much worse than last time. The commander waited for her to speak. Finally she said, "Our cell did not believe in violence. The goal was to win people to the cause, then take over by non-violent means."

"Revolutions are seldom non-violent," the commander said. "They exist and operate outside the law."

"But the law on Alphorion is rotten with bribes and governmental debates that go nowhere!" Philippa burst out. "I remember my parents talking about having to raise bribe money, like it was part of life! And then, to be paying to support a dying planet while officials argue endlessly and do nothing—"

The commander put her fingers together. It was a small gesture but it silenced Philippa. "So parliamentary procedure takes a long time."

"They'll argue forever and never make any decision about planets becoming self-governing."

"Maybe not in my generation." The commander nodded. "Why should that be the same for yours? The process is slow, but it's designed to protect the innocent."

Philippa sat back in her chair.

"The cells were badly divided after the abortive attack, and many of the members resigned or scattered. One of the leaders, Miguel Arcaro, was able to obtain false identification papers and leave

Alphorion as a crew member on a trade vessel. He was traced to this planet, and there the trail has ended. I am here to ask whether or not he has contacted you or tried to employ you in his interests or aid?"

Long habit kept Philippa's face blank. Inside, her thoughts clashed and jangled. *Did you kill people, Miguel? Were you really protecting me when you did not tell me this, or protecting yourself?*

Her eyes closed. She could see Miguel's face, when he told her that his heart belonged only to the planet.

I don't know what the truth is, or what's truly right.

She opened her eyes. "It really upsets me, what you say about the cell committing violence. Maybe I'm lucky I had to leave." She sighed. "Miguel did send me a message, from Gandria, but I did not send him an answer. He didn't send a second one, and I don't know where he is."

Silence stretched for a time, then the commander laid aside the flimsies she'd had in hand. "In that case, there's nothing more for us to discuss, is there? Thank you for your time, Miss Bidding. I'll walk you to the waiting area."

The commander was Philippa's height exactly, the girl realized hazily, as they walked to where her father was still waiting.

Philippa gazed at his smooth face and cold eyes, wondering what she would say, then the commander spoke from behind. "Thank you, Director Bidding, for allowing your daughter to meet with me. She's obviously a very bright young woman, and I believe that one day she'll understand our position. See that she has a choice of the best schools!" And to Philippa, as she shook her hand firmly, "Good minds like yours can work to the benefit of everyone. Remember what I said!"

FIFTEEN:

Dance Night

Zach's mother touched the controls, and the screen went dead. "All right, Zacho. You're through for today. If you're feeling sick, then I suggest you stop and visit Dr. Tourni on your way out. And if this is some kind of scam to net surf time, I'm disappointed."

Zach sighed, rubbing his clammy hands on his pants. "I'm fine, Mom, and I'll concentrate. Let's go on. No scams! I promise!"

Dr. Yamoto smiled but did not move to reactivate the test program. "You've been acting edgy ever since the Tourni girl—what's her name, Clea?—poked her head in. If there's a problem between the two of you, maybe you should find her and get it settled."

Zach stood up and stared at the flatpic of Galahad. "No problem with Clea," he said. "There is one with some others, though." He smiled back over his shoulder at his mother. "Soon solved, I hope—"

They were interrupted by the comm-link. Zach watched his mother answer. "Yamoto here." She listened for a short time, then raised a questioning face to Zach. "*Do* we have Sean Matthews and Arkady Davidov here for an experiment?"

"Yes," he mouthed the word.

Dr. Yamoto studied Zach's earnest face, then said slowly, "The boys are participating in an experiment involving my son, Mr. Santori. I will authorize it, if—very well. If they finish early, they will be sent to the yard! Yes. Good-bye." She said, "I hate to lie blindly, Zacho."

Zach took a turn about the room. "I'd like to tell you about it. Or about what happened—" He stopped and thrust a hand through his hair impatiently. "I'm not making sense! It's like this. I have to ask the others first, and the time to ask is not now. Maybe soon."

"Don't fret." His mother stood up. "I've plenty that needs doing. Stay here. Solve your problem. If you need help, ask. Don't sink too deep trying to be independent! We don't need two kids in the soup."

Zach laughed, distracted for a moment from his thoughts. "Tris?"

Dr. Yamoto nodded, her eyes crinkled with amusement. "Apparently he and his group have signed out enough vid equipment to keep them doing trade-off service for ten years. Your father had a talk with Director DeVries last night—but don't mention that to Tris and his friends."

"I know nothing!" Zach said.

His mother winked. "I'm going to check on my

patients early, which means I might actually get a lunch today." She went out.

Zach sat down at the desk and buried his face in his hands.

Arkady looked up suddenly.

"Here, hand me that." Sean held out greasy fingers.

"Quickly," Miguel put in. "It's threatening to skid again."

Miguel was holding several engine parts together as Sean carefully fitted the gyroscope in.

"It's Zach," Arkady whispered.

Sean glanced up and impatiently knuckled his black hair out of his eyes. "Any words?"

"No."

Sean grunted. "If you ask me, this toroid current is worse than useless. You get just enough to make you jumpy, and nothing that can be used—" He remembered his audience then, and glanced at Miguel.

Miguel was tightening bolts with a makeshift tool. He glanced up in time to catch Sean's suspicious look. He smiled slightly. "Tell me this only: Is Philippa part of your mysterious connection?"

Arkady said nothing. Sean nodded slowly.

"Good." Miguel went back to work.

Clea had deliberately selected a seat at the back of the biology lab, in case any of the gang showed up for the class. She felt relief ease her entire body when Philippa slid quietly into the next seat. She glanced past Noriko Wilder's short black hair to the robot tutor, which was talking serenely about microbes, then tapped out on her portable terminal: *How did it go?*

Philippa turned on her terminal and punched: *My part is over, no problems. Anything from the boys?*

A shadow crossed their terminals, and the girls looked up to see Zach plopping into the seat behind them.

Zach leaned forward and typed quickly on Clea's terminal: *I haven't heard anything, and neither has Will.* He directed a questioning look at Philippa, who then pointed to the message still glowing on her screen. Zach nodded and added: *Let's meet at the shift change at the IRC.*

Arkady squinted up at the hazy sunlight as Sean fitted the casing onto the scooter, then he stood up and wiped his hands down his ruined clothes. "Past midday. Oblitt's class soon."

"Oblitt'll be the last in line for our hides if this wreck doesn't start," Sean said grimly as he dropped into the driver's seat. He paused and exchanged looks with Arkady and Miguel, then he flicked the toggle.

There was a pause, then the rising whine of the engine, which nearly drowned out the boys' loud cheer.

The three of them settled into the hoverscooter, and the craft rose on its beam. Sean maneuvered it delicately out of the grove of trees, then slowly back up toward the road. "Vibration. Hear it?" he asked as they reached the road and began picking up speed.

"Take it slow. Take it slow," Arkady murmured.

"I'll watch behind," Miguel said, hefting the seat

support they'd twisted into a crowbar shape, and slapping it against his other palm.

"Why are *you* so moody?" Paul asked grumpily, frowning at Will.

Will turned and looked down at his stepbrother, who appeared more nervous than Will had thought possible. Will felt an urge to smile, but did not. "Some friends are late, is all," he said.

"That's no reason to fidget around like that," Paul said irritably.

"Sorry. I'll go wait in the den."

"You're going, aren't you?" Paul demanded. "To the dance."

"Of course!"

"I mean, with anybody?"

"With a group." Will shrugged slightly.

"But—"

Will paused in the doorway, looking back.

"Oh, nothing."

The door hissed closed behind Will. Through it, he heard a distinct grumble from Paul: "A *stupid* social system."

"Stop here," Miguel spoke suddenly.

Sean slowed the hovercraft carefully, but did not turn the engine off. He and Arkady looked back in question.

Miguel pointed out the bubble of the Spaceport Dome, which glowed in the light of the setting sun. "I'll take it from here."

Sean sighed. "We can run you to Transport."

"This is a small colony, and you two have taken enough of a risk. I'll scout around, and if there's any way to get off the planet, I'll find it. Meantime, you might get yourselves into the city before dark. The engine's getting ragged, and your would-be rammer is still loose."

Arkady nodded soberly. "There's that."

Miguel dropped the makeshift crowbar into Arkady's lap, and hit the back door switch. Before he got out, he grinned at Sean and said, "We could use a driver like you."

He was walking down the road before Sean could voice a reply.

"They're safe, " Clea said.

Philippa nodded. "And on the way."

She and Clea cut the connection, then Philippa returned to her room. A quick glance down the hall showed her parents' door still shut.

Philippa returned to a careful perusal of her wardrobe. "They're safe," she murmured to the quufer lying on her pillow. The creature *quued* back at her.

"They're safe, and coming, and nobody got caught, and my parents were left with nothing to say to me. By some miracle, everything is all right— except why do I feel so nervous?"

"Quu! Quu!"

"You're right!" Philippa laughed. "Because it's left me with all the explaining to do, plus a lot of questions." She turned back to her wardrobe, and kept mulling over her clothes, making critical comments for the quufer's benefit, until the loco announced at her door: "Callers, Philippa dear."

Philippa slipped into the last choice and left the room. Zach, Will, and Clea were waiting in the Yamoto car. "Ah, my beauty!" Zach greeted

Philippa. "Moonlight and starlight combined!
Enemy defeated?"

"You mean the League investigator or my
parents?" Philippa asked ironically, sitting down
next to Will. "Answer: both. Has anyone heard
from Sean or Arkady?" She looked at the other
three faces. "No? Same as me then: *on the way.*"

Zach laughed and started driving.

Paul parked the family two-seater carefully, and
walked to the front door of the DeVries' dome. A
moment later, there she was. Paul stared, mesmer-
ized, as Daphne greeted him. He was dimly aware
of lots and lots of lace and gold and long, shining
magenta hair. She had dimples when she talked,
and she smelled like roses.

"I said, how are you, Paul?"

Paul made a supreme effort, and launched into
his meticulously planned date program. "Good
evening, Daphne," he said. "I am delighted to have
your company for the evening. If you are ready to
go, I have the family hovercraft waiting outside. My
parent and stepparent waived their claim to the
vehicle in our honor, so we may depart whenever
you desire. I hope you had an interesting day today.
I certainly had one; my studies were combined with
duty in the most informative manner as I was
assigned to the lab at the tidal generator. . . ."

He kept talking as he escorted her to the vehicle,
then drove them the short distance to the
Entertainment Center. They parked and walked to
the brightly lit multi-purpose room, which had been
decorated with rainbow-diffraction streamers, but
Paul scarcely gave them a glance. He strove to be
interesting and adult as he gave her a detailed

description of the lab experiments that he and Dr. Petrov had launched recently.

They found a place to sit down, and Daphne was still smiling when he stole a glance at her. *Why, this isn't so hard after all!*

Feeling exultant, he eagerly embarked on a detailed outline of the master plan for tidal measure and prediction.

Philippa was dancing with a tall, blond newbie whose interests seemed to be entirely taken up with sports. She replied smoothly and automatically when he prefaced each description of his triumphs with a question, "Have you ever played . . .?"

Over his shoulder, Philippa suddenly saw Sean and Arkady enter the crowded room. She saw them scan the dancing teens. Sean's face brightened in a quick grin when he saw Will and Clea. A moment later, he saw Philippa, and lifted his fingers in a brief "all's well" salute. Arkady's light, cool eyes found her next, but he only nodded a greeting. Then the movement of the dancers around them took the entire gang from her view.

"What, freeball? No, I've never tried that," she said, registering a question from her partner. As he began giving her the rundown on a long game he'd won, she concentrated inwardly. *Zach's pleased. Clea's—nervous. Why? Will is sad—*

Vertigo from spinning made her stop. When she opened her eyes, her next thought was: *There's no longer any danger, so am I spying?* Philippa knew how much she hated her own lack of privacy. This was something new to think about, and maybe discuss with the others.

The dance ended—there was Zach. "My dove, it appears you're free!"

Philippa saw Will staring at a bright head across the room. "That's why he's sad," she said suddenly. "Do you think it's wrong to feel his feelings?"

"Wrong?" Zach looked where she was gazing.

"That's why Will's feeling that way. It's her." Philippa saw Zach study Daphne DeVries, who was sitting stiffly in a chair, listening with a fixed expression to Paul Riedel talking earnestly, rapidly, and without a pause.

"Oh-oh," Zach said. "I recall now! Ages ago. At the beach. I thought Mam'zelle DeVries had cast down a gauntlet at our Will's feet."

"Cast down a what?"

"A gauntlet," Zach repeated, grinning. "Ancient signal that a duel to the death over some lady's fair name was about to begin."

"What was a gauntlet?" Philippa asked, choking on a laugh.

"Some type of armor. Or was it an armament?"

"Amazing." Philippa shook her head. "You spend so much time trying to skate work, just to waste hours over old and meaningless archives."

"Never say it's work." Zach looked aghast.

"No, never," Philippa murmured soothingly.

Zach grinned. "Shall I be a knight errant? I'll have to abandon you." Philippa gave him a push, and watched him thread his way among the laughing, dancing teens to Daphne's side. He bowed to her, then bestowed an apologetic grimace on Paul, who watched open-mouthed as Daphne promptly stood and held out her hands. Soon Zach and Daphne were swirling dashingly into the crowd, each one showing off a flair for fancy steps that soon had a small audience of kids watching and applauding.

Philippa also watched, grinning. *Now for my own unfinished business.*

She turned to survey the crowd again, spotting Sean's black hair above most of the other heads around him. As she watched him, she felt his attention sharpen suddenly.

Her feet started in his direction, but as she registered what he was staring at, she stopped. Meanwhile, Sean moved steadily until he was standing before a small, black-clad figure with short dark hair.

Philippa watched Noriko Wilder lift her chin and stare up at Sean. They exchanged a few words, then they were dancing. Philippa felt her own insides twist peculiarly. Deliberately, she turned away.

Arkady was standing nearby. He said, "Your friend is on his way."

"Thanks." Philippa felt hot. She pushed her dampened hair away from her forehead. "What happened? We were worried."

"We'll have to talk about that later," he answered briefly.

"You were covered today."

"So Zach said."

Philippa rubbed her forehead again. The current was blank from Arkady, which she found nearly as unbalancing as Sean's fascination with Noriko, and Will's sudden surge of hope.

"I think I'll look for the eats," Arkady murmured, moving away.

"Arkady," Philippa said.

He stopped and turned. His light-colored brows rose in question.

Her usual easy social chatter seemed to have deserted her; she said in a rush, "Are you angry with me?"

"No."

He was still waiting. She said, "That night, when we talked. You never told anyone about that."

"You never told anyone what I told you. About myself and Anna."

She shook her head. "No."

"Did you think you're the only trustworthy person in the world?"

She understood it, the hurt he'd felt finally. Then it was closed off again. "Well, yes," she said, her voice shaky. "Because I was, at least in my world!"

"There's that." Arkady smiled, a question in his eyes. "Your Miguel's all right."

"But not for me." *And that, apparently, now goes for Sean as well.*

Arkady nodded soberly. "I expect it would be the same," he said, "if I saw Anna again." He gave her another brief smile and lost himself in the crowd of kids.

SIXTEEN:

Together Again for the First Time

"You may be a gobble-tongue and a waffle-brain, but you dance divinely," Daphne said sweetly in Zach's ear.

He twirled her deftly under his hand. "Oh, to be slain by a coldhearted beauty! Who's next on your list?"

"Who says I've got a list?" she asked with a laugh.

"But—" Zach gave her an astonished stare. "Surely you don't mean I'm the only one you intended to mop up tonight? I should say, cruel, cold hearted beauty!"

"You mean poor Paul?"

"No. If you ask me, I think he's secretly relieved," Zach whispered, for once, if only momentarily, serious. "But if you hadn't intended to deep-freeze his brother, then you are a mean one!"

"Deep-freeze?" Daphne repeated. "I suppose that's one way of looking at my reaction to his oh-so-flattering attention to a lowly newbie."

"If you think," Zach murmured in her hair, "he thinks you're a lowly newbie, then you have been eating too many of Grumps's protein crunchies. They are known to addle the brain."

"Huh?" But before she could ask him what he was talking about, Zach let go of her hand and swept a low bow. "I surrender to a higher claim!" He glanced up at Will as if scanning the heavens, put Daphne's hand in Will's big paw, and disappeared into the crowd.

Will gave Daphne a funny grin.

He's shy! Amazement made her silent for once. Will didn't seem to need any words; he folded her tenderly in his long arms, and they moved into the group of dancers. She noticed with further surprise that, though he did not seem to be able to run well or to surf, Will Mornette was a fine dancer. Still, at the end of the dance, she looked up into his face and saw tiny beads of dampness on his brow. "How about something cold to drink?" she suggested, pointing to the chairs. "Tell me! Would I like a low-gravity dome world?"

Will grinned at her. "Sure—well. If you like pure air, and don't like crazy weather—" He stopped, drowned out by shrieks and howls of laughter. Daphne and Will turned to see some of the other teens jumping away from something near one of the doors.

A moment later, a shrill noise resolved into the familiar chattering of theskies, and three of the creatures raced into the room. One jumped on top of the buffet, sending fruit-crush splashing across the plates of cookies. "Temper! Emper! Emperor-temper-terror-terra!" The theskie looked about, its orange eyes excited, then it leaped down. Cookies went flying across the floor.

Sean and Will went after the creatures, and the theskies were promptly rounded up and ejected. Daphne helped the drudge-workers clean up the worst of the mess. She was surprised when Zach Yamoto appeared and gave her a hand at righting a small table and picking up platters. He straightened up and shoved his hair back. "Did you hear what those theskies were saying?"

Daphne shrugged. "The usual meaningless mess of words. Temper and emperor were two words I made out."

"Emperor." Zach sighed. "Aren't the young kids supposed to be having their party in the big vid hall?"

"Oh!" She laughed. "You think the young kids let the theskies in?"

Zach grimaced. "Led by my brother Tris. Ever since he started that stupid vid about kings and pirates, he's been acting like both. I'd better go straighten him out." He disappeared in the crowd.

Knowing that this was her father's first major function as recreation director, Daphne felt a bit like a hostess. She walked slowly around the room listening. The party sounded a lot more exciting now; on all sides, kids were explaining about theskies to the newbies. She heard, "Don't be surprised to step out of the shower and find one holding your towel!" and, of course, "I heard that two kids were sitting on the hill, kissing, and a theskie popped up between them and started quoting theorems!"

"Yesterday I heard that one, but it was quoting Plato," a husky female voice said next to Daphne.

Daphne turned and saw Noriko Wilder looking skeptical. On her other side, Sean Matthews laughed. "I heard that when I first got here, and there wasn't anyone but scientists around. For them, it was quoting von Kleinmark's rock opera."

"My mother warned me about scientists," Noriko said.

"Being one?" Daphne guessed.

Noriko's dark eyes gleamed. "Yours, too?"

Daphne tossed her hair back. "An artiste! She's on tour now—Sybilla Wentworth."

"Vids?" Noriko asked, looking interested.

"*Only* high drama." Daphne laughed. "Sean, didn't you once—" Daphne stopped when she saw that Sean's attention was elsewhere.

Noriko also looked up. Sean was staring across the room, his face intent. Before Daphne or Noriko could say anything, he muttered, "Be back in a tenner." The two girls watched his tall body making its way through the crowd. He joined Arkady at the door—a moment ahead of Will Mornette. All three went outside.

"I'll lay you a wager," Daphne said to Noriko, "that if we were to walk out after them, we'd find Philippa Bidding in the center of an admiring circle. Maybe Clea Tourni as well."

"Philippa. Gorgeous one. Light hair?" Noriko gestured.

"That's the one."

Noriko gave a slight one-shoulder shrug. "First claim, I'll look elsewhere."

Daphne slung her hair back impatiently, remembering Will's shy smile just a little while ago. "It's not that, I don't think. I don't know how to explain it! But they all do it—Sean, Clea, Zach. Arkady, too. Not Philippa. She's too exclusive for even that much! They play and flirt and talk with everyone, but then suddenly," Daphne said and snapped her fingers, "it's like, 'later for you airheads' and they close up and go off somewhere."

Noriko's lips quirked. "We'll see if he comes back."

Paul watched Daphne and the short girl with the black hair walk back to the refreshment table in deep conversation. He turned away.

Suddenly he was tired of all these older kids, all talking and dancing and flirting and acting as if he was invisible. Earlier, he'd felt triumphant, walking past the rooms where the kids his own age were having their children's party; now he drifted in that direction. Of course, he had no hope that they would notice him, either. *How was I supposed to know she'd want to dance?* he thought morosely. *What an* abysmal *social system!*

"Oh—there's Paul," he heard a hiss.

Paul looked up to see Jehanne standing farther down the corridor, waving at him excitedly. He walked a little faster, and when he reached her, she grabbed his arm and yanked him into one of the small vid-viewing rooms. "Are we allowed in here?"

"*Shh!*" Jehanne said. "Look. We need to know. You helping us or not?"

"Jehanne." Tris winced. "It's not like he has to decide or die." Tris waved at Mik and Tank before saying, "We've gotten in too far, and we need your help. We can do our end—we're learning—but the comp work is going to be beyond us.

"It seems every single kid in Ambora knows about the vid, and they're counting on us to finish it," Tris went on. "With a waiting audience, it'd be stupid to give up! We'll be rich in no time! But we've got to have help, and I still refuse to get the Thirders in. So?"

Paul felt relieved—and shy. "I'd like that, I think."

"So it's settled!" Tris smacked his hands, grinning. "Let's—"

"Tristram!" The voice was Zach's, and it sounded nearby. "Where are you? We need to talk about some theskies, before I melt your pelt!"

"Whoo," Tris said uneasily. "I wonder if there's an exit out back?"

When the theskies ran through the crowd, the shrieks and yells of everyone at the dance added to the creature noise drove Philippa to seek some quieter space. She felt uncomfortably cramped inside. Finding one of the side doors open, she slipped out.

There was a low railing around a small terrace. Philippa wandered to the rail and stared across the park area to the big moon, which crested the uneven black line of the far mountains. The air was cool but still, and Philippa rubbed her arms slowly, taking deep breaths.

Her emotions felt strange. Strong and clashing, like those temple bells she'd heard once on a field trip. She flexed her fingers, wishing there was something she could hold or press or twist. *Miguel's gone. And I've lost Sean.* She watched the quiet moonlight rilling in the pond, and thought of her cold house. *Isn't there anyone for me?*

"Philippa," a timid voice said.

Philippa turned. She recognized Clea Tourni's

thin body lit by the glowglobes near the door.

"Oh, joy," Philippa said with all her usual irony. "I suppose I'm splashing all five of you with my self-pity?"

"I saw you leave," Clea said. "You didn't look happy. Is it Sean?"

Philippa waved a hand. "I don't know. Sean, and Miguel, and did I do the right thing by protecting him today? But then I couldn't say anything, could I, and not drag you and the others in? They were trying to help. The P.L. commander said Miguel was involved in a terrorist conflict. I guess mostly I don't want to believe that Miguel could betray the ideals of the Leffies. . . ." She hesitated. "I guess I don't want to think my first hero—first love, really—is responsible for the deaths of twenty-four people."

Clea said softly, "I heard Arkady tell Zach that he and Sean had been ready to drive him to Gandria and abandon him. They changed their minds—they seemed to like him."

"Their opinions being so important." Philippa shook her head. "Sorry, Clea! I guess I'm not great company. Maybe I'd best go home."

She jumped over the low wall and walked quickly across the cool, wet grass. When she reached the front pathway, she saw a tall figure standing there, staring up at the brightly lit windows of the Rec Center. Yellow light gleamed in waving black hair, outlining a straight shoulder in a dark boorman.

Philippa's steps slowed; she was not aware of her footfalls making any noise, but the young man's head turned quickly. She saw green-glowing eyes at the same moment he must have seen hers.

"Miguel!"

He closed the distance between them, the light from the windows touching the side of his face. She saw an expression of surprise and concern. "Hello, Philippa."

"What are you doing here?" Her voice came out sounding sharp, and she amended it quickly. "I mean, I thought Sean and Arkady saw you to safety."

"'Safety' is going to be a relative term for the rest of my life, I think," Miguel said with a quick smile. "As luck would have it, I was walking on a flat section of road—no cover in sight—when a craft came along. Of course, the driver stopped and offered help. She believed my story about a broken-down scooter, and she assumed I was going to this dance, as apparently everyone else is tonight." He shrugged. "She went out of her way to drop me off. Seemed simpler to go along. I was just trying to decide whether I dared duck in and look for a city map so I could figure where to go next."

"You were lucky," Philippa said. "Or maybe *she* was lucky."

Miguel's head angled up sharply. Philippa saw his mouth tighten, and points of gold light from the windows reflected in his eyes as he stared down at her. "Someone told you about Arlicot Island."

"Why didn't you tell me?"

"Let's not stand here, all right?" he asked.

She pointed to a section of low wall sheltered by a line of trees. They walked side by side in silence. Philippa's racing mind was distracted by scraps of music and laughing voices drifting out into the night air, and by Miguel next to her, his empty hands at his sides. She sat down, hugging her arms tightly.

"I didn't tell you," he said, standing before her,

"because it seemed to me that you'd left the old life behind. It seemed you'd decided, or were about to decide, to make this planet your home. Also," he said and smiled quickly, his head to one side, "and you probably won't like hearing this, but I'd forgotten how young you are. You'd seemed older on Alphorion."

She gave a bitter, shaky laugh. "Tell me what happened."

"It was a team action, our first. Alynn and I sought unity among all the Leffie groups, and it turned out the Sigalls just wanted more bodies for a fight. The original plan was mine. Go in, take hostages, make our broadcast, then slip out fast. No one to be hurt. Prove we could do it if we had to. Sigall's gang never intended to follow my plan, it seems. They produced the weapons—and some of our people took them."

"Did you?"

"Not at first." Miguel paused, looking away at the still waters of the dark pond. "You were probably told that twenty-four people, tourists, and League security guards were killed. You were probably *not* told that nearly as many of us died. Most of our casualties were unarmed, untrained in combat, from our group. You were probably also not told that nearly twenty of those tourists who died were killed by a couple of young P.L. recruits who panicked. They thought they saw Marc Sigall get on that elevator, right after shooting down four of their company, and they blew it off the cables."

Philippa wiped her sleeve across her eyes. "You said 'not at first.'"

"When I saw both sides going crazy, some shooting to kill, I picked up a gun dropped by a dead guard. I used it to get as many of our group as I could gather to the harbor and away."

"So you killed people, too?"

"No. I wounded three guards—shot their feet from under them."

Philippa shivered. "But that means you knew what you were doing. You *do* know something about guns and combat."

Miguel nodded slowly. "Just because I knew what I was doing doesn't mean I wanted to be doing it."

Philippa was silent.

"I told you the truth, there in the safe house, that I needed time to think," he went on. "Despite my beliefs concerning non-violence, when I found I had to take action, it felt . . . right. In a situation of 'shoot or be shot,' the people on the other side became mere targets, and I didn't want to talk, but to win. This makes me, in some ways, no different from Marc Sigall." Miguel put a hand on her chin and made her look up at him. "If you do go back to Alphorion, Philippa, you'll be meeting a lot of people like Sigall and like me. You'll have to decide what to do, and afterward, decide whether you've done right."

Philippa took a deep breath. "Did you do right?"

He smiled faintly. "I don't know. But if I keep questioning, maybe I'll figure out the answer." He looked toward the Rec Center door, which had opened to let out a noisy group of younger kids. "I'd better go."

She stood up, resolutely controlling her voice. "You might be stuck on Gauguin for a while. I heard—at the party—that the crew was full on the transport ship, and another isn't due for some time."

"My grandfather used to say, 'The best way to think is to go fishing.' I'll be all right." His fingers just brushed her cheek. "Why don't you rejoin your friends?"

"Take care, Miguel," she whispered.

"I owe you one, linnet. *Au revoir.*"

Philippa watched him walk away until he had disappeared among the trees on the other side of the park. Then she slowly wandered back to the Rec Center terrace, without really thinking about where she was going. There, she found Clea still waiting.

"I hoped you'd come back," Clea greeted her nervously. "I went after you, but when I saw you talking to someone, I didn't want to interfere."

Philippa was touched by the other girl's concern for her—and for her privacy. "I'm all right," she said somewhat huskily. "Thanks."

The door opened, and Zach sauntered out. "At last I've found you! My beloveds." He opened his arms.

"Oh, no," Philippa said with an unwilling laugh.

"Note how cleverly I've sidetracked the other guys into making points with the newbies, leaving you two incandescent creatures to me."

"You mean you had no luck with the new girls?" Philippa shot back.

Zach sighed. "Why is it that no one will go out with me?"

"Because you call them things like incandescent without fair warning," Clea told him, trying not to laugh.

Philippa surreptitiously wiped her eyes, thinking: *Clea wants us all to be happy.*

"Would you prefer fair candle, bright angel, searing torch?" Zach offered theatrically.

"Glaring bulb, young lamp, clip-on campflash . . ." Philippa said in a drippily romantic voice.

Zach and Clea both laughed. Philippa thought, *Zach as well.*

The door opened then, and Will came out. He was followed by Sean and Arkady.

All six of us.

"Something wrong here?" Sean asked.

"Just another unsuccessful Yamoto moonlight flirtation attempt," Zach shrugged.

"Three of you together made my current home in," Arkady said.

They looked at one another. "This," Zach said portentiously, "is seriously weird. We can keep ignoring it, and end up counting sheep in one another's dreams."

"You said something about learning to control it," Arkady said.

"Not control. Some techniques for shielding. I'm trying to learn that, and I'm trying to learn something called focus. Maybe I can get you in for sessions with my mother. She's the best here, and she won't say anything. Or ask, if that's what you want."

Philippa nodded slowly. "I'd as soon not be shipped off to an exclusive resort for the incurable elite. At this point, I think my parents would love any excuse."

"Won't happen, Pippa-my-Prune," Zach said. "You're not alone in this."

"Right—and my father outranks yours," Sean said grimly.

All six of us together. Philippa felt, cautiously, the

other aspect of the common bond. Not the intrusions but the sharing. She said nothing, but inside her, something eased a little. *I'm not alone*.

Will Mornette felt the tension in the group, and turned to Sean. "What happened last night?"

"What happened was, some toroid slime-crawler tried to ram us. Came out of nowhere while we were skirting the city on the eastern road."

"Maybe it was a steering problem," Clea suggested hopefully.

"Twice?" Sean kicked at the wall. "And we couldn't chase 'em, or investigate—I nearly killed us just trying to stop."

"Someone after Miguel, maybe?" Will asked.

Arkady said quietly, "Maybe. Unlikely, though. He's in trouble with the law. They don't ram civilians."

"Not that I ever heard." Zach nodded in agreement. "And you were in your dad's official vehicle, right, Sean?"

"Yeah. Nobody in the P.L.'s gonna ram it. Someone else outside the law might. We'd just been talking about how everyone knows it by sight."

"Going to report it?" Philippa asked.

"Report what? That we took a midnight drive for no reason, two hours outside the city, and some mystery person tried to ram us and disappeared?" Sean grimaced. "What happened last time we tried to report something weird? . . ." His voice trailed off.

Arkady completed the thought, "—an abandoned hunter's campsite marked by bloodstains. Which no one could find later."

"Back to our starting point." Sean struck the wall

lightly with his fist. "There *is* something going on."

"And you think these incidents may be connected," Philippa said. "Leaving us with only what, where, how, and why."

"Tell you what I think," Will spoke up, looking around at them. They were all giving him their attention—Sean looking fiery-eyed and ready for action, Arkady cool and determined, Zach thoughtful, Clea nervous but equally determined, and Philippa bright-eyed and tense. "Sean's right," Will started. "We're back where we were a week ago. So let's start again, and do one thing at a time."

Zach slapped Will on the shoulder. Will could feel Zach's energy, trying to lighten the general mood. "The tall man's right. Shall we set a date for another try on our model of the plateau city?"

"Tomorrow," Sean put in, his hand on the door. "Tonight, let's dance."

Will thought of Daphne, and agreed fervently.

Zach lunged forward and linked arms with Clea and Philippa. "All right, my plums, so you haven't fallen for the great Yamoto charm. How 'bout just pretending, for a minute, so's to establish my reputation with these newbies?"

They all entered the dance hall, laughing.

Here's a sneak preview of *Visions From The Sea*, book number four in the continuing PLANET BUILDERS series from Ivy Books.

Inside the marine research station, a portable terminal slid and crashed into another screen. Noriko balanced on her toes, lunging forward in time to catch a printer before it fell to the floor.

When the swaying stopped, Noriko saw Philippa turn silently right back to the comm-link. Beyond her, Daphne was still, just staring.

"Help me grab up all these little chips I just lost," Noriko said. "Sure glad they make these buildings flexible."

Daphne uttered a strangled-sounding laugh. "Guess they do, huh?"

"Here, hand me the yellow chips first," Philippa said, "I'll try to get us on—"

Philippa's voice died away, as if she were concentrating on her work. Noriko reached up to hand Philippa the parts that she had collected. It was then that she saw Philippa sitting very still, the little silver tool poised in the air above the comm-link. Philippa was gazing straight ahead of her as if listening to something very, very far away.

"Philippa?" Daphne said cautiously.

"*Miss* Bidding!" Coordinator Withard was at the door, looking angry and disheveled. "This is not the time to panic."

Philippa looked up blankly. "There's trouble at the outstation."

Withard's anger was replaced by worry. "The comm-link? A call—" She stopped, looking at the half-dismantled comm-link. "*What's this?*"

Philippa made a quick gesture. "I'm trying to repair it. The first big quake knocked it out in the midst of a call. But I know that there's trouble at the outstation, and someone has to get there fast."

"What do you think you're doing! Get out of here!" Withard's voice rose. "This is why we kept you away from the machinery downstairs, so that no damage would occur—"

Noriko felt cold fingers on her wrist, and turned to see Daphne nodding slowly. "Will. He's in trouble. It's like I can hear him calling," she whispered. "Like seeing that city . . . it comes in and out, but"—she drew a very shaky breath "—I really think this is *real*."

"It is," Philippa started. She jerked when Withard's fingers dug into her arm, but her attention was on the comm-link.

"Get this room cleaned up, then get out of here—*now!*" the woman snapped angrily.

Noriko saw Philippa cast one look out the big observation windows at the boats bumping against the dock in the choppy waters, though her hands were still busy among the wires. It was clear that another essential task had arisen—though *how* it had arisen was a total mystery.

When Noriko saw Philippa look at the boats, she made her decision. *Doesn't matter how she got that message about the outstation. She knows*

*she's right. And if Daff is somehow getting the
message as well—*"Where's the location map?"
she asked.

*The map Kessler set aside for his backup crew
is there on the log table. Shows where today's
drops were planned.*

Noriko nodded, reached—paused when she
realized that Philippa's words had not come to
her through her ears, but right into her head. She
blinked, feeling strange, and looked at the blond
girl. Philippa glanced at her covertly.

I'll question that later, Noriko thought then.
Out loud to Daphne, she said, "Want to help me
lock this down?" She touched the map.

Withard paid no attention to them. "I've got to
call Central," the woman was repeating.
"Someone has to know about these quakes!"

"*She's* the one in a panic," Noriko muttered to
Daphne as they took the stairs down. She heard
Daphne give a humorless laugh, then Withard
was forgotten as Noriko led the way to the boat.

Noriko was no expert with computers and the
like, but she knew a lot about the various types of
hovercraft. She looked over the controls, started
the engine, and cast off the moorings. "Want to
try raising the other boat, then check around for
the first-aid gear?" she asked Daphne as she
guided the boat away from the dock.

Daphne was braiding her long hair hastily. She
tucked the bright magenta ends into the neck of
her boorman and bent to look through the storage areas. "First-aid stuff here!" she called.

The redheaded girl bent over the communication controls, then exclaimed, "Ah! This is *just* like the 'link my mother has—uh, had—in her aircar at home." Her fingers jabbed, then paused. She looked up at Noriko. "According to this readout someone recently tried to raise the other boat. Maybe Dr. Nils? Anyway, the other boat isn't responding."

"Let's go," said Noriko.

She ran her hands over the controls, getting a feel for the way the boat moved over the water. Soon it was skimming at the highest speed she dared, which meant several needles were just shy of red.

Noriko turned to face into the wind, fiercely enjoying the speed the boat was making. This craft was much more powerful than the little excursion boats she'd handled back home on Epsilon, but she kept it steady.

She also kept an eye on the power: the gauge read half, and she had no idea how much power would be needed to get them out to the islands and back.

Daphne joined her after a while.

"Boring field trip so far, eh?" Noriko grinned at her.

"Cor-*ro*-sive!" Daphne touched the wrist-cam on her arm. "Well, I didn't mean to bring this, but at least it's safe! We'll know as soon as we can get it into a viewer." She looked up again, her face solemn. "Twice now, I've heard Will. In my mind. It's like he—he's thinking about me.

Remembering things we've done. I see myself through his eyes, and I . . ."

Noriko saw the other girl wince. "Hearing how much he cares about you," she suggested, remembering Zach's brief words to Philippa: *Just got calls form Sean and Clea . . . Nightmares about you and Will and Arkady.* Calls from Sean and Clea—Noriko forced her thoughts away from Sean.

Daphne nodded. "But it's not just that—even though I feel bad about some of the things I've said and thought lately. It's how worried he is, and not just about me. If this is real"—her gray eyes gleamed with tears—"he doesn't have much time left. He thinks he's going to *die*, Noriko! We've got to get to him soon!"

Die? Noriko felt a moment of panic, swiftly followed by anger and the urge to take action. She glanced at the location gauge, the map, and the power. Then she clenched her jaw. "So what if we swim back," she said. "If we have four to swim, it'll make a party."

She slapped the control all the way to max. The boat seemed to buck and leap forward, as if trying to take flight.

"Hang on," Noriko shouted. "We're gonna have a hot ride!"

Will peered up through the thinning smoke. Though he could see absolutely nothing but steam, smoke, and choppy dark green water, his mind produced a sharp memory image of Svirle's black outline. Thinking about the volcano sent menace curling like new flame through Will's insides.

Will tightened his grip on Arkady's belt and looked through Arkady's mask. Arkady's eyes were still closed, but at least he was still breathing steadily.

Will looked around, wishing he could see *anything*. The seawater on his globe made the steam and smoke drifting across the water seem thicker. He did not want to take off his globe, through; these giant bubbles that welled up from time to time below might be filled with noxious gases.

Will looked at his readout bar. Air wasn't the problem; they still had plenty in their air packs. What did worry him was the steadily rising water temperature, which meant lava was seeping up in ever-increasing amounts. It was not the water itself that worried Will; he knew that the seawater temp would not increase over one hundred degrees, well within the range of protection their suits offered, but what if lava came up right under them?

But where could they go? Will could not see beyond twenty meters in any direction, and the bubbles seemed to be rising on all sides.

Will activated the suit's call signal for the fourth time, then he gripped Arkady more securely.

"Will."

It was just a murmur, but Will twisted about

and looked into Arkady's globe, relief washing through him like a cool bath. Arkady was awake.

"Suit's hot,"Arkady mumbled.

"Water temp is going up," Will said. His voice was shaky with relief, but he didn't care. "I've got Paul's comp going on auto, clipped to my belt. If it doesn't fritz out, he should get some primus readings."

Will saw Arkady wince and try to shake his head. "My ribs,"Arkady said. His voice was hoarse, but a little stronger. One of his hands moved lightly over his midsection. "Ribs. Cracked, I guess. What happened?"

"I think a massive magma leak came up right under us," Will said. "A rock caught you—a rock that was headed for me." He briefly described his own impressions, ending with the Stingers.

"Stingers?" Arkady repeated.

Will could not surpress his own excitement, now that Arkady was conscious again. "They were swimming close to us but not touching us. But when I tried to go in any direction other than east, they got *real* close—bumped me twice! Anyway I went east, and as soon as I realized they weren't going to kill me I remembered your wrist-cam. When I grabbed it to shoot them they disappeared."

Arkady was shaking his head slowly. "I thought . . . they're so dangerous."

"They are. Three deaths that I know of. One on the first deeps-survey team, and two more that were classified, but my dad told me anyway."

"Any colonists missing?"

"I think that's why this was classified: *no one* had been reported missing."

"Strange," Arkady repeated, obviously making an effort to speak.

"All of it's strange," Will said. "I've sent four signals to the boat. Think you can swim? More to the point, where should we swim to?"

"My head hurts," Arkady said softly. "Try the mental current?"

Will hesitated, then said: "I believe I got through to Pippa once. She was intent about something, but I think she heard me, all right. Since then," he hesitated again. "Well, since then it might be stupid and wishful, but I've been thinking at Daff. What's more, I keep feeling she's heard me."

Arkady said merely, "Any words?"

"No. None with Pippa, either."

"If my head clears a little . . . I'll give it a try," Arkady said.

Will watched Arkady stretch out slowly until he was lying flat in the water. Except for one grunt of pain, Arkady said nothing, not even when a huge bubble rose and popped a scarce ten meters away, sending brownish steam drifting toward them across the chopping water.

Despite the suit's insulation, Will felt the temperature rise. The lava seepage must be increasing. He closed his eyes, thinking about last night. Seeing Daphne laughing, reaching once to touch his hand. Her warm fingers. The way her lips curved just before she smiled.

He rocked suddenly as a huge bubble popped very near. Steam boiled off the water. When it thinned, he saw scorched seaweed and dead fish floating amid small chunks of black rock.

"Hot seaweed stew," Arkady joked hoarsely.

Will looked at Arkady, whose eyes were closed again. He was about to speak when he felt the *thrum* of an approaching engine. He flicked on his globe light, turning in all directions. A moment later a huge shape loomed, forming into a boat.

Will blinked up through the steam and salt smears on his globe. He just recognized Noriko at the controls—and there next to her was Daphne, her bright braid swinging. He could see her shouting his name as she threw something. A rope ladder snaked out and landed between the two boys.

"Arkady !" Will called. "You go first."

Arkady said nothing, but Will could tell by the way the other boy gripped the ladder and slowly eased himself up that he was hurting badly.

Will followed close behind, but as soon as they were at the top, Arkady gasped, "Will. Pippa says there's trouble at the station."

Daphne reached for Will's globe. Will clumsily helped her get it off, then there she was, her voice midway between laughter and tears. She grabbed his head and pulled it down and gave him a long, sweet, and salt-tasting kiss.

"I *heard* you, I *heard* you!" she said over and over.

Will hugged her tightly against him.

"What is it, Arkady?" Noriko said sharply, reaching to help Arkady open the face plate in his globe.

"He says the outstation is in trouble," Will said past Daphne's shoulder.

"Pippa," rasped Arkady. "Thought current. Danger."

Noriko jerked around. "We're low on power," she said. "Have to crawl back to the main station as it is, and you look like you need a medic now."

Arkady shook his head slowly. "Outstation— Bryce. Fast as we can."

"To the outstation it is," Noriko said. With a rising whine, the boat lifted and sped out into the steaming seas.